ENFORCER

A SEATTLE SHARKS NOVEL

SAMANTHA WHISKEY

D1059863

ENFORCER

A SEATTLE SHARKS NOVEL

Samantha Whiskey

Cover Design: Mayhem Creations

ISBN# eBook:

978-1-946356-94-9

ISBN# Paperback:

978-1-946356-95-6

ALSO BY SAMANTHA WHISKEY

The Seattle Sharks Series:

Grinder

Enforcer

A Modern-Day Fairytale Romance:

The Crown

To anyone who has ever had a celebrity crush

CHAPTER 1

RORY

HERE I AM, again. I glanced down at the bruises marring the knuckles of my right hand and muttered a curse. Coach was going to fucking kill me. Fighting on the ice was one thing but in a bar? Yeah, I was pretty much screwed. Given the fact that I'd been sitting here since early this morning, my guess was he not only knew but had decided to let me stew.

My temper had been sitting at a simmer since I'd been handcuffed. My ass was numb from the hard metal of the bench, my mouth tasted like something was slowly dying in there, and I smelled like bar smoke and stale beer.

This was definitely not the image my publicist had been trying to cultivate.

"Jackson, Rory," the cop called out from outside my cell, glancing up from his clipboard.

"That's me," I said, standing.

"You look like shit," a familiar voice said from next to the cop.

"I'll give you a second," the cop said, holding an autographed Seattle Sharks hat in his other hand.

That's how Gage got back here.

"You would too if you'd slept here." I snapped at my best friend, gesturing to the cells all around me. At least I'd had my little 10X10 to myself. Perks of clearing $8 million last year, I guessed. Gage lifted one black eyebrow and shook his head.

"I wouldn't be in the jail cell. Oh, wait. That's right. *I'm* not."

I folded my arms across my chest. "I'm not in the mood for your shit."

From the corner of my eye, I saw at least three of the other guys—who'd been brought in way after I was—leaning forward against their bars. Not that I could blame them. Gage and I were two of the best-paid and well-played Seattle Sharks—the hometown NHL team. "Just get me out of here," I ordered, lowering my voice.

"Why would I do that?" Gage asked. "At least if you're in here, I know you're not out there getting in trouble. You do realize Coach is going to bench your ass, don't you?

I sighed, my shoulders drooping, and rubbed my hand over my forehead. "Yeah, I know."

"And you do realize that this is the first year we could actually win the Cup?"

"Yes."

"And you realize that you're on your seventeenth strike of his 'three strikes and you're out' policy?"

"God damn it, yes, I know that," I hissed.

"Then what the fuck were you thinking?"

"The guy was an asshole," I said with a shrug.

"So you hit him."

"He tried to hit me first." And the minute he'd swung, hell the moment anyone swung, they all became *him* in my mind.

Gage shook his head and looked at the ceiling like he was hoping God would come down and save him. "Un-fuck-ing-believable." A couple of deep breaths later, he finally looked at me again. That amazing control was what made Gage a fantastic grinder on the ice. My temper was what made me the Seattle Shark's best enforcer, but it was also my biggest liability. "Grow the fuck up, Rory."

"Working on it," I told him.

"We're ready," Gage called over his shoulder, and the cop reappeared. A few quick motions and he had my cell unlocked.

"You're free to go," he said.

"Thank you..." I glanced at his nametag, "Officer Jonas."

About ten minutes, a few signed papers, and one plastic bag with my belongings later, we were in Gage's car, pulling into Seattle traffic.

"My truck is still at the bar," I told him when he made a turn in the opposite direction.

"We're headed to my house. Bailey picked up your tux —so remember to thank her—and if we're fast, we can still make it in time."

"Make it in time..." My brows lowered. What was I forgetting?

"If you forgot, you'd better pray that Coach comes for you because Bailey will *kill* you on Paige's behalf." He wove in and out of traffic, his nearly-dangerous driving at odds with the small booster seat in the back of his car that established his dad status.

Paige. Gage's fiancée's best friend and the current subject of most of my fantasies lately. *Okay, all of my fantasies.* She was fucking perfect—petite, gorgeous, with a body that begged to be stripped out of those super-serious suits for some super-serious fucking. She was brilliant, and not just in a 'yeah-she's-smart,' kind of way. No. She was Ivy League and the only girl I considered *out* of my league.

"Paige's fundraising gala," I muttered, rubbing my hands over my face.

"Bingo," Gage said, crossing three lanes of traffic for the exit.

"Fuck, I forgot that was tonight. It's not like every other Shark won't be there. She won't notice one empty seat."

Gage pointed to the dash clock. "Red carpet is at five, which means we have exactly an hour to get ready and get there. And yes, when it comes to you, she absolutely will notice."

Right. I did promise to autograph all those sticks. Shit.

"Okay." I ran through a quick mental schedule. At least I'd have time for a shower, so I wouldn't show up smelling like I'd spent last night and the better part of today in a drunk tank.

We pulled into Gage's driveway as my cell phone rang.

"It's Coach Harris," I groaned.

Gage killed the engine and slapped my shoulder. "Good luck, with that. Your tux is in the guest room when you're ready."

"Thanks, man."

I answered the call as Gage shut the door, leaving me alone in the car.

"Coach."

"Jackson." His voice was soft, which I knew meant he was way more pissed than when he yelled.

"I have no excuses and I know it's not enough to apologize," I said, leaning my head back against the rest.

"You're damn right you don't, and it's not. Look, the guy agreed not to press charges—"

I breathed a huge sigh of relief.

"—but I can't exactly look like I'm letting you off the hook on this one."

"Yes, sir."

"You're way past the age where you should be pulling this shit, let alone two months before playoffs when we're an actual contender."

"Yes, sir."

Now it was his turn to sigh. "Look, Rory. You're good. Damn good. You and I both know it. But this has to stop. There's a line between being a playboy with a temper and getting your ass thrown in jail. It looks bad on me, the team —hell, the whole franchise. You cannot be the face of the Sharks if you're wearing orange, you get me?"

"Yes, sir," I repeated, waiting for the other shoe to drop. My no-trade clause ended at the end of the season, and for the first time in my career, apprehension ran up my spine that I wouldn't be in Seattle next year.

"I have to bench you this weekend."

"Coach—"

"No, you sit there and listen. Take this weekend and figure out what the hell it is you're doing, and how much you really want to be a Shark. This can't happen again."

"I understand."

"If it does...then we'll have to take the hit to the roster and bench you for the season. And then..."

"Yeah, I get the picture."

"Clean up your image. Hire a better publicist, or hell, just listen to the one you have. But for fuck's sake, stop acting like a hormonal teenager with something to prove."

"Got it, Coach."

We hung up, and I made my way into Gage's house, going through the garage door. We made the same salary, but we couldn't live any more differently. Where I had a two bedroom penthouse loft downtown, Gage was up here on the hill with a huge house, complete with painted pictures on the refrigerator and an array of toys in the living room. He had something I didn't, and didn't know if I'd ever be lucky enough to have—a family.

"Hey, need some water?" Bailey asked from the kitchen as I walked by.

"That would be great, thank you," I said as she handed it over. The diamond on her left hand looked good on her—so did the small swell of her belly where another McPherson was growing. "Where's Lettie?" I asked, looking for their precocious four-year-old.

"With Gage's mom," she said with a smile.

"Wow, you look gorgeous," I told her, taking in the arrangement of brown hair on the top of her head and sweeping black dress.

"Thank you. Now you'd better get dressed before I'm forced to kick your ass." She nodded toward the guest bedroom, and I saluted her with the water bottle, draining it on the way to the shower.

I washed the bar and jail grime off, thankful that I kept a small toiletry kit here for nights I was too drunk to drive after our weekly poker game. Ten minutes later, I had clean hair, scrubbed skin, and brushed teeth.

Wrapping a clean, white towel around my waist, I walked into the guest bedroom and stopped dead in my tracks.

"Oh!" Paige said, her mouth a delicious O shape. Her eyes ran hungrily down my bare chest, and I resisted the urge to flex.

Guess she did notice me after all.

Her red hair looked soft enough to touch, and the hue of

her red lipstick against her pale skin made me wonder what those lips would look like wrapped around my cock.

Do not think like that about Bailey's best friend.

What the hell was I supposed to think about when she was standing there in a bathrobe? One simple tug of the belt and she'd be naked—all milky white skin and pert breasts.

Shit, if I didn't get ahold of my thoughts, they'd make themselves known soon. The towel wasn't going to hide much.

"I'm so sorry," she said, her voice sweet and clear. "I meant to be out of here by now." She tugged on her lower lip with her teeth and I cursed my semi-hard on that was going to be a full one soon.

"No problem. I enjoy finding partially-clothed beautiful women." I smiled, and she blinked quickly for a moment.

Then something marvelous happened—she stood straighter, her chin rose, and she morphed from shy, delicate Paige, to Vice President of CranBaby Organics Paige, calm and collected. Damn, I couldn't decide which was sexier.

"I'll just grab a dress and change in the bathroom."

I followed her gaze to two dresses hanging on the closet door. One was black and elegant with a simple scoop neck and lace overlay with cap sleeves. It was refined and screamed perfect for the Paige I couldn't touch.

The other was red, strapless, and would hug every one of her delectable curves. It was the dress for the Paige that might ogle my bare chest.

"The red," I suggested, my voice gravelly.

Her green eyes widened subtly as they found mine. "You sure?"

There was a palpable zing between us, the mark of hot as hell chemistry that I'd never experienced on a level like this before.

Bailey's best friend.
Bailey's best friend.
Bailey's best...oh, fuck it.

"I'm sure. Wear the red." I forced a smile and hoped it was charming instead of horny as fuck. "And save me a dance."

"Okay," she said softly, taking the dress and damn-near running from the room. Since I stood in the doorway from the attached bathroom, I couldn't help but wonder exactly where she was going to change...or why she'd left so fast that I'd wanted to check for fires.

"Down boy," I told my dick.

I found my tux and started to dress, trying—and failing —to keep my mind off Paige and how she was going to look in that dress later.

She wasn't the girl for me. She was smart, put together, driven, and straight as an arrow. Hell, I doubt she'd ever even parked illegally. She was the kind of girl you built a house for, not the kind you hailed a cab for after a marathon of sex. Hell, I couldn't even get my hands on her, not with her connection to Gage.

She was off limits in every way.

Well, every way but my fantasies...and I had a feeling her ass in that red dress was going to make more than one appearance there tonight.

CHAPTER 2

PAIGE

#7: Sleep With / Fuck Rory Jackson.

The number on the dirty-girl bucket list Jeannine had made Bailey and myself make over cocktails one night burned in my mind as red as the dress I wore. The dress Mr. Jackson *himself* had chosen for me. I'd known the modest black gown was the option I should've selected but when he'd pointed to the red something inside me sparked, and I *couldn't* say no to him. It may have had something to do with the white cotton towel barely hanging onto his perfect hips—complete with lickable v lines and a rock hard abs I wanted to trace with my fingertips.

I shifted anxiously in my seat next to Bailey in the back of the limo I'd arranged to pick us up at her house and did everything I could *not* to look at Rory. He sat next to Gage across from us, staring out the window with his brow furrowed like he was mentally trying to hold the world together.

What on earth could the playboy Shark have to worry about?

Like a magnet, the sight of him tugged at my chest,

begging me to smooth the wrinkle away and tell him whatever it was couldn't be that bad. The man had everything from a celebrity athlete status to an endless supply of puck bunnies and fantastic parties to attend plus a job he loved and was damn good at. Just thinking about him on the ice sent warm shivers all over my skin and I licked my lips unconsciously.

Rory blinked and flipped his gaze to me, catching me practically drooling over him. I jerked my head around so fast I nearly hit Bailey with my nose.

"Paige?" She asked, placing a steady hand on my shoulder. "You all right?"

Blood rushed to my cheeks, and I straightened my back. "Perfectly fine."

Bailey arched a knowing brow at me, but when I briefly glanced toward the two gorgeous hockey players sitting merely a foot from us, she nodded. There would be time to talk later and damn if I didn't need her to shake some sense into me. My undeniable urge to dive across the seat and straddle Rory to check off number seven on the list right here and now was almost as consuming as the knowledge that I absolutely *couldn't* do that.

Our limo finally pulled up to the Four Seasons, and I sucked in an encouraging breath. We were next in line, just like everything else in my life. As Vice President, I loved being the behind-the-scenes brains of CranBaby Organics. After all, it was my family's multi-billion dollar corporation, but I'd yet to really feel comfortable with the more public aspect.

This black-tie gala was more than public...it was press-worthy. Dozens of flash bulbs went off as I prepared to get out of the limo, careful to keep my good-girl covered. The last thing Dad needed was to see my panties splashed on page one of the social section of the Seattle Times—not when I was this close to finally taking over as president.

Seven years of working my way up from the bottom floor, earning my position within my father's company—despite the disbelief of outsiders—and my dream was finally coming true. Not only would I be the head of one of the largest global family products companies in the world, but I'd also be in a position of power to make a real difference, and I knew just where to start—Seattle's homeless and underprivileged. For years I'd dreamed of revolutionizing the concept of the shelter. I wanted to make them bigger, better-stocked with food and supplies—really transform the system into a working outsource program. Give those who'd lost everything an honest chance and not the glossed over photo-op they had now.

Dad had always been generous, making donations to any charity I recommended, but this concept was my baby, and I couldn't wait to have the resources at my disposal to bring it to light.

But I knew with the power would come sacrifice, and not just at events like tonight. I couldn't very well live a wild life while heading the world's most wholesome family corporation. In fact, the contract I'd sign in three months had a morality clause that said exactly that. In order to be the face of the company and my own dream organization, I had to put every dirty, scandalous whim behind me. For good.

Not that I ever did anything scandalous, anyway.

One more quick glance at Rory and my breath caught in my throat. Jeannine had been right, one night with him would totally be worth the risk.

Forcing myself out of fantasy-land, I checked to make sure the flash drive was in my clutch as we pulled up to the entrance. Matt Donaldson, the newest Oscar contender in Hollywood, was throwing this little shindig on behalf of Water.org, and maybe if I could get these plans into his hands, I'd have a chance at teaming up for state-of-the-art water filtration systems for the shelters.

"Thank you all for coming," I said, glancing at Bailey and Gage but determined not to look at Rory one more time. If I did, I might lose the concentration I so desperately needed right now. "The signed gear will bring in a ton for the charity. I owe you all, big time."

Gage smiled and reached out to squeeze Bailey's hand. "Anything for you, Paige," he said and a fissured cracked in my chest. I was overjoyed for Bailey—she'd gotten her dream man, and with a baby on the way, her life was pretty perfect—but I couldn't help but feel as if those things would never be in the cards for me. Not with the life I was expected to lead as President. And while it had been my dream take over, it was more clear than ever what I would be giving up to achieve it.

I smiled at Gage who lovingly smoothed his hand over Bailey's tummy. I'd gotten ready over at their house so I wouldn't have to walk the red carpet alone, but with Rory only a foot away, and the lovebirds even closer to me, I was starting to wonder if I should've sprung for separate cars. The heat in this one was enough to melt the cool, calm demeanor an event like this demanded.

A final deep breath and my hand was on the door.

Here we go. Now don't fall on your face.

I tossed my dark red hair to give it an extra boost and stepped out of the limo, my black heels surprisingly stable on the red carpet as I tucked my small clutch under my arm, hoping I looked more confident than I felt. I'd gone an inch higher in the heel department thanks to Jeanine's advice, but so far hadn't fallen on my face, so I was declaring victory.

Camera's flashed in a succession of bursts, and the paparazzi shouted from behind two thick, golden velvet ropes that sectioned off the red carpet leading into the entrance. *Damn, Matt Donaldson knew how to play to his audience.*

The technique was smart, business-wise. Pump up the A-listers the second they walk into the hotel, stroke their egos, and then watch as their deep pockets loosen. Clever *and* all for an excellent cause.

Add to it that he'd invited the entire starting line of the Seattle Sharks, our resident NHL team, and it was enough to spin the head of any donor—male or female. Their picture was blown up about twenty feet high to my right, and it more than drew my eye. Lord have mercy, those men were dripping sex, confidence, and built like Greek gods. Gage, Warren, and Rory had been featured in Sports Illustrated as the sexiest slice of ice this side of...anywhere, and yeah, they were. *Especially* Rory.

My entire body clenched just looking at his picture, but knowing he was right behind me reminded me just how long it had been since it had clenched anything besides my vibrator. The fact that he'd come on my behalf—or rather Bailey's—made my thighs heat in a delicious way that made me want to turn around, grab his hand, and drag him to one of the penthouses upstairs.

Get a grip on yourself!

"Ms. Turner!" I paused half-way to the entrance, plastered on my good-girl smile, and found the pap who'd called for me. "How long has CranBaby been a supporter of Donaldson's charity?" The short man had his camera poised in the perfect position to record every flaw I had.

I glanced at the venue, grinning as I caught sight of Jeanine waiting for us at the entrance. "We've recently heard about the cause and understand the extreme need behind it. I'm here to show my support and hopefully learn more to help spread awareness and see what CranBaby can offer."

My fingers played with the clasp on my clutch nervously, but I halted the movement as soon as I was conscious of it.

I'd been in the limelight since before I could remember, but it didn't mean I liked it. It came with the family name and the old-as-time corporation we ran. I'd learned early on that someone is *always* watching. And while the whole world was entertained by the mistakes of others, our stock prices were not.

"There's a rumor that you're being groomed to take over your family's corporation, Ms. Turner."

He's baiting you.

I kept my smile firmly in place. "Was that a question?"

A general laugh went through the pap line.

Good job. I wasn't one to make a mistake. I'd been a good girl all my life. Teacher's pet, straight-A student, and the perfect daughter who would rightly take over the family company in a mere three months. The future I'd always dreamed of would be mine—and the expected public appearance that went with it.

"Given that you are such a family-driven business, have you given any thought to how you'll find time to start one of your own once you do take the throne, so to speak?"

I swallowed, and tilted my head at the older reporter, doing my best to hide the fact that he'd just tap danced across my rawest nerve. Brian Watercomb finished his questions to my right and moved toward the entrance. "You know, I think Brian Watercomb and I are about the same age, and he's poised to take over his father's shipping empire any day now. Did you ask him the same question? Or did he get a pass because he's a man?"

The reporter stepped back, his neck flushing the same color as the carpet.

Good. Asshole. I flashed a playful smile to let them know my feelings weren't hurt. "Now, anyone else have a girl-only question they'd like to ask?"

"Who are you wearing?" another pap asked.

"That's one I don't mind." I ran my hands over my fitted number, loving the way the ruched fabric hugged my curves. "Prada." I winked.

"Red is definitely your color," Rory whispered in my ear, his breath shooting a thousand chills across my skin. He was close enough to touch me, but his hand remained casually in his pockets.

"Rory!" Another pap shouted, and I jolted out of my trance that his nearness had put me in. "When did you take an interest in Donaldson's charity?"

Rory shaped his lips into that picture perfect smirk he'd mastered and motioned his head to me for the briefest of moments. "Anything Ms. Turner supports is worth investing in."

I swallowed hard, another flush raking my skin. He could've given Gage all the credit or even Bailey, but he'd put the focus right back on me.

"You two are friends?" The reporter pushed.

I grinned, taking the reigns. "I'm a die-hard Sharks fan." A secession of whoops and claps rang through the crowd, and I flashed Rory a smile. "Now, if you'll excuse me I'm needed inside." I waved quickly, leaving Rory and Gage to answer more questions about their upcoming game. Bailey followed me as we walked the rest of the carpet until we'd made it inside.

"You did great!" Jeanine said, looping her arm through mine and squeezing me close to her model-perfect body.

"Dad might not be too happy with how I answered that family question."

"You're about to be one of the youngest female CEOs of a multi-billion dollar corporation. I think he knows you need to stand up to the bullshit. Now, what do you think?" she asked, her hands gesturing to the scene before us.

The banquet room was filled with circular tables draped in gorgeous cream-linens, waiters in black ties serving top-shelf liquor, and of course, half of Hollywood's elite. The room dripped with classic calla lilies and crystals that looked like water droplets in tasteful, but opulent arrangements.

"The room is lovely, but what about the food?" I asked, gently nudging my best friend.

"Yes, I'm starved," Bailey said, lightly touching her tummy.

"Didn't you eat before we left?" I teased.

"Ha ha." She glanced down where her hand still touched her stomach. "I swear I'm in a constant state of hunger now. It has to be a boy."

Jeannine and I took a moment to smile at her, pure love and maybe just a tad bit of jealousy radiating from us over her insane happiness.

"What?" She asked when she noted the looks on our faces.

Jeannine broke first. "There is plenty for you, Bailey, *and* that little Shark you're growing. Plus, the food is mine and therefore exquisite."

"Do you need to check on anything?" I asked.

She shook her head and smiled at one of the actors as she led me to our table. "Nope. I had Rafael come in tonight to run service. My menu. My recipes. My food. My night off."

"I know you better than that."

"Well, if they fuck it up, then all bets are off. I didn't bust my ass for that third star to let them ruin it. But for now, I'm relaxing."

I took in her skin tight blue dress and matching heels. "Relax, indeed."

Before we reached the table, she turned me, both of her manicured hands on my shoulders. "I'm loving the red." She eyed my dress. "Am I finally starting to rub off on you?" She asked, a sly grin on her face.

"Nope, that'd be Rory," Bailey answered before I could, resulting in a jaw drop from Jeannine.

"Did you *sleep* with him? Is number seven the first to be crossed off the list?" Jeannine practically bounced in her heels.

"Could you keep your voice down?" I asked, glancing around to make sure Matt Donaldson wasn't within hearing distance. "Of course I didn't. He happened to be at Bailey's the same time I was."

"And how does that get you into this smoking hot dress your father will surely pitch a fit over?"

"I was wondering the same thing," Bailey said. "Spill."

I sighed. "He pointed to it, and I chose it. No big deal." My girls laughed, and I couldn't help but join in. "Why is that so funny?"

"Because he's on your dirty girl bucket list!" Jeannine squealed. "He wanted to see you in this number." She pointed at the Prada. "He'll be totally down to help you with the list. Just ask him. Plus, he's a fantastic choice for a one night stand."

"Stop," I hissed, eyeing Bailey for help.

She shook her head. "I'm sorry, but I agree with her."

"Traitor!" I gaped at her. "You're the most sensible one of us all! You're supposed to have my back when Jeannine takes these wild ideas of hers too seriously."

"It's just sex," Jeannine said. "Chill out. Besides, I'm fully in favor of you letting your hair loose before your dad stuffs it behind a habit."

"Great, now you're making nun jokes, too," I mumbled, wishing I'd never told her that I felt like I was about to become the next member of Sister Act.

Bailey chuckled, glancing over her shoulder where Gage, Rory, and Warren talked to half of the other Sharks across the room. The amount of good looking men in tuxes was enough to get every single female within breathing distance pregnant. "Rory is one of those men that is down for absolutely anything," she said. "And while that is fun, it also gets him into trouble. I think it might benefit *him* to sleep with someone like *you*."

The worried look Rory wore earlier flashed behind my eyes. "What do you mean *trouble?*"

Bailey lowered her voice as if he might overhear us from fifty feet away. "Gage actually picked him up from jail earlier. That's why we were almost late."

I gasped, covering my hand with my mouth as my eyes darted to him. His back was to me, but I knew his short cut blond hair and muscles anywhere.

"What'd he do?" Jeannine asked.

"Another bar fight. The man has a temper," Bailey answered.

"That's not a shocker. He's ferocious on the ice," I said.

Jeannine nudged me. "Ohmygod you are so strung up on him. How are you not pursuing this right now?"

"I'm here for business."

"You're always everywhere for business, Paige," she said and sighed. "And soon that is all your life will be. If you don't live a little now, you might not ever get the chance." She spotted a server over my shoulder and hurried toward him. "That's not how I wanted the plates arranged!" She said as she stormed toward the back of the room where I assumed the kitchen was.

"Don't listen to her," Bailey said, squeezing my wrist.

"I'm not." That was a lie. Jeannine's words were sitting cold and hollow in my chest, the fear of never getting a taste of anything exciting before I signed my life away chilling me to the bone.

"Sure," she said, rolling her eyes.

"Okay," Jeannine said, popping up behind me. She motioned toward the table we stood next to. "I have a confession."

"You slept with Rafael," I said.

She rolled her eyes. "I never screw my employees. Especially not the good ones." Her forehead puckered and I started to get worried.

"What did you do?" I raised a singular eyebrow, but let it go. Whatever Jeanine had planned, it would be harmless. She was the wild one out of our pairing, but she'd never do anything to embarrass—

Fuck. My. Life.

"You didn't," I hissed at her as I saw my name card on the table.

Paige Turner. And directly to my left. *Rory Jackson.*

"Why isn't he sitting with the rest of the Sharks?" My

tone came out too close to a whine, and I sucked in a deep breath.

"Gage is sitting next to Bailey. I figured he'd want his friend Rory there too," Jeannine said innocently.

"Uh huh." I slit my eyes at her.

"Speaking of sitting," Bailey said, hurrying around the table to her spot, releasing a deep sigh once she was parked.

"Just call me Cupid," Jeannine said with a smile as she took her seat to my right.

"Just call you dead," I snapped but sat down. I eyed the room for a waiter. "What does a girl have to do to get a drink around here?"

Someone tinkled ice in a glass to my left. "Scotch and soda, right?" Rory said, setting the drink in front of me but didn't take his own seat.

My lips parted, but no words came out. *Speak woman!* "Thank you," I said once my breath had returned to my lungs. "How did you know what I liked to drink?" I took the glass and sipped. Tonight would call for multiple scotch and sodas.

"I *have* seen you almost every weekend for the past few months, you know?" He tilted his head.

He was often over at Gage's when I was there visiting with Bailey, but that didn't mean we were all together enough for him to notice details about me like what I liked to drink. Did it? I eyed his still empty chair. "Are you going to stand the whole night?" I asked, laughing slightly from the nerves bundling in my tummy. When he towered over me like that it made me think of all the ways in which I'd love to climb him.

Rory licked his lips, reaching over me and taking a quick sip of my drink. "Later. Right now I have some sticks to sign."

I arched an eyebrow at him. "The sticks you were supposed to have signed last week?"

He shrugged, pointing at the drink. "That's my apology for being late." He took a few steps away from the table, winking at me. "Don't worry, Red. I won't let you down."

I watched him walk away, admiring the way his tux pants fell around his hips. *Good lord my panties will melt off if he sits next to me all night.*

"Holy fucking hot," Jeannine said, smacking my arm. "If that isn't reason enough—"

"Stop," I cut her off and took another large drink. My cheeks were still on fire from his gesture.

"Paige, come on. Just promise me that you'll *try*. For once, stop thinking about what's best for the company or your family, and think about yourself. You're about to sign your freedom away, so just try to enjoy it first." Her eyes were wide with her plea.

I sighed, mostly because she was right. Maybe it was the scotch talking, but I finally shook my head, incredulous that she'd won. "Okay, if he actually comes back without an adoring puck bunny attached to his hip, I will..." I sucked in a deep breath. "Attempt to make number seven happen."

Sex. With Rory Jackson. A hot, hockey stick-wielding god of the ice. A gorgeous, famous, panty-melting notorious bad boy. Sure, it sounded great in theory, but in reality, I wasn't sure I had what it took to even make the first move. At least he wasn't a complete stranger, that had to count for something right?

An hour and a half, two scotch and sodas, and one delivered flash drive later, Rory took his seat next to me. He spread his right hand out on the table, clenching his fingers into a fist before fanning them out again.

I chuckled. "Signing them in groups over a week would've been easier on your hand."

"True but there is no challenge in that." He grinned before ordering his drink.

"Thank you, again," I said, suddenly losing all the witty banter I had built up in my head with his body so close I could feel the heat from his skin.

He waved me off and tapped my place card. "Paige *Turner*. When you see it written out like that it's..." he laughed.

"Mom has an incredible sense of humor."

He set the card back down and chuckled. "I can relate."

"I think Rory is a strong name." And I wondered just how strong he was? Enough to hold me against a wall and make my eyes roll back in my head? How hard would it be for me to get him into bed? His well-advertised colored past suggested it shouldn't take more than a few hints. Plus he *had* just said he'd never let me down.

Are you really going to do this? Yes. Wait. No. I shook my head. *Yes.*

Crap. I'd shaved and done some general landscaping, right? Right.

He held his glass out to me. "To funny and not at all ironic names."

I scooped up my drink and clinked it against his.

My eyes followed his tongue as it dragged across his bottom lip, and suddenly I *wanted*. Wanted not in a "gee, that'd be nice," way but an "I need that more than dinner," kind of way. Good God, how could I get that in my mouth? I'd never seduced anyone as renowned for being a wild man before, but I was a grown woman about to take over a multi-billion dollar company, I could do this.

Your pep talk suggests otherwise, my nagging inner-prude said. I shut the bitch up with another drink. Perhaps I should approach it like a business deal—an asset I absolutely needed to possess—cut throat and direct was always the key to success.

Matt Donaldson came on the stage before I could choke my proposal out. He drew everyone's attention as he spoke about the cause and made a few jokes at the expense of his friends. He nailed the speech, creating a perfect balance between need and emotion, successfully wringing out another donation from myself as I assumed everyone else as well.

"Thank you all for coming. The drinks stop when you say, and the music starts now," Matt said.

Applause broke out as he descended the stage and wove into the crowd to mingle. A band played a few moments later, starting the night off with a peppy jazz number.

"You'd better nail him, or I will," Jeanine whispered in my ear. Then she shoved me, flinging me into Rory's massive, muscular frame.

He caught me easily. "Whoa, are you okay?" His hands stroked down my arms, sending whips of electric current through me.

"I'm so sorry," Jeanine said. "I'm just clumsy." She stood as I regained my seat. "I have to go check on the rest of tonight's food, and I just fell right into you, Paige. My bad! You have fun!" she ran off before I could physically beat her to a little blonde pulp.

Rory's fingers lingered on my arms before he let me go. The loss of his touch was like stepping away from a warm fire. "Would you like to dance?" I asked Rory, taking my courage by the lady-balls.

He set his drink down and pushed back from the table, offering me his hand.

Wow. That actually worked. I took it, the heat from his skin somehow touching every inch of mine.

We made it to the center of the dance floor and though there were stars all around me—including two of People's Sexiest Men Alive from the last five years—I couldn't take my eyes off Rory. He radiated sex. The peeks of scars beneath his unbuttoned collar gave him a dangerous vibe that had me more than ready to run my tongue down the raised skin. He was rough on the ice—an enforcer famous for initiating and finishing fights while simultaneously helping his team rack up wins. And tonight I wanted him to win *me*.

Every time my conscience came to surface, I shoved her back down with the reminder that I only had three months. That was it. Then it was the boardroom and the nun habit. But not tonight. Tonight I was dancing in heels with Rory Jackson.

I wrapped my arms around his neck, my heart pounding as he settled his hands on my hips and moved us to the music.

He smelled like soap and cedar and mouth-watering man. The way he moved made my body bend in ways that seemed impossible for the dress I wore, but somehow, I didn't end up flashing anyone. Maybe it was because he kept me firmly pressed against his body, which let me feel every hard plane of muscle he possessed.

So this was desire. Want. Lust. I wasn't stupid. I knew this wouldn't turn into anything more—not with the way he rotated women on a weekly basis—no matter how much I thought there was more to him than his bad boy status. More than his looks, his muscles, his raw sex appeal drawing me to him, but right now it was his incredible body that held me captive. Like I was flipping fuses in my head, I shut down all the logic I used in the boardroom and instead gave my body control.

As the band segued into a slower tune, Rory motioned to leave the floor, but I pulled him in closer.

"One more," I said, slightly breathless. I knew I had to act fast before I lost all my nerve and my last chance at number seven.

Rory smirked and snaked his arms around my waist, bringing his lips to my ear.

"What's your angle, Red?"

I jolted slightly against him, pulling away from his chest to meet his eyes. They were sharp as a hawk. He didn't miss a beat, so I damn sure wouldn't miss mine.

"I want you," I forced out, my eyes wider than the sultry demand required. Okay, so I wasn't a born seductress, but damn he made me feel like maybe I could be.

He cocked an eyebrow. "I picked up on that. But we've been at Gage's with drinks flowing enough to need guest rooms for the night, and you never made a move. My question is why now?"

"Is it that hard to guess?" *Don't look further. Don't make me look deeper.*

"Sometimes. You're a smart woman, and I don't see any delusions of love flashing behind those green eyes of yours. So again I wonder, what's your angle?"

I shook my head. "How do you know I'm smart?" Because this now seemed like the stupidest thing I'd ever done. Turning myself into a puck bunny over a fucking list.

No. A groupie would follow him around and beg for sex. I would not do that. This was a business offer. He'd either accept the proposal or not.

"Anyone who is about to head up a world-wide organization has to be more than sharp."

"First with the drink and now you know about my career?" I tilted my head at him, curious as to what all he noticed from afar.

"Do you think I'm completely oblivious?"

"Of course not." I smirked and took a deep breath, allowing my breasts to graze against his chest.

He hissed but pulled me closer. "Is it the trophy? Bailey tell you fucking a Shark is the way to go? Because I'm nothing like Gage," he warned.

The direct question, paired with the way his body tightened against mine, fueled my drive. That and the way his lips moved when he dropped the f-bomb like it was a promise, was hot as hell.

"No." I slipped my fingers into the hair at the base of his neck like it was the most natural thing in the world to touch him so intimately. "I like to keep my personal life private. I don't want you for your money, or your status, and I have zero inclination toward becoming your girl."

He narrowed his eyes at me. "Well, those are all great reasons for why you *don't* want me. What's the reason you do?"

I tugged at my lower lip with my teeth. "Look at you."

His gaze drifted along my features like I was a puzzle he was trying to put together.

The music stopped, and we broke apart, our eyes locked in what was the most intense eye-sex of my life.

In fact, I was pretty sure he'd make me come on the dance floor if he kept looking at me that way.

"I'm so glad I found you!" Jeanine said, swooping in with a grin. "You left your key card at the table." She pressed the cards into my hand. "Penthouse," she said with a wink at Rory. "Knock him dead. I want details," she whispered in my ear before dancing off.

My mouth opened and closed like a fish out of water, my body at war with my very reasonable brain. His tongue slipped out, wetting his incredibly full, wickedly sexy lower lip, and my body won the war. How could it not?

I slipped the extra key-card to the room inside his jacket pocket, not asking, or even waiting for him to answer. The words wouldn't come out anyway. I made sure to put a little extra swing in my hips as I clicked off the dance floor and out of the banquet room, high-fiving myself once I was clear. I hadn't fallen or made an ass out of myself. *Yet.* I stopped in front of the elevator bank, my own access card in hand. My heart raced, the anticipation and adrenaline mixed inside me and forced my brain to go beyond rational. I'd never been so direct in any of my relationships before, but I suppose this wasn't a relationship situation.

I wasn't a starry-eyed Cinderella, and my shoes weren't glass. I wasn't stupid enough to think this was my happily ever after. No, this was my incredible *now*. This, if he agreed, would be the memory I kept locked inside my vault for when my boring, acceptable future husband couldn't get me off anymore. I grinned like a lunatic at my uncharacteristic behavior. I was good at business, and that's what this was. Dirty-girl business. And I hoped like hell he'd become an investor.

CHAPTER 3

RORY

I FLIPPED the key card over my knuckles as the elevator rose to the penthouse floor.

What the fuck are you doing?

Maybe the real question was: what the fuck was Paige thinking? The floors dinged by as I rose, each one bringing a new thought.

Ding. Paige was a flawless beauty, the kind you didn't see in magazines—they'd never lower themselves to be judged by their looks because she...

Ding. ...was brilliant. Her brain never slowed down. Hell, she outmaneuvered men in business as if they were driving bumper cars at the Indy 500.

Ding. She could have any guy she crooked her finger at, which hadn't been *any* since she'd started coming around Gage's place to hang with Bailey. Why me?

Ding. There were a thousand reasons it shouldn't be me.

She wasn't a one-night stand kind of girl, no matter how she swayed her ass after that little offer she'd laid out downstairs. No, she was the woman you meticulously planned dates for, strove to keep her interest, and then drove onto Relationship Ave with as quickly as possible before taking the Engagement onramp to Matrimony Highway. I, on the other hand, was a total one night guy.

The floors sped by, and I rubbed my thumb against my forefinger, grappling with a decision I should never have been presented with in the first place.

She was champagne, and I was beer.

She was Chanel and Dior, and I was Under Armour.

She was responsible where I was reckless.

Ding. The doors opened directly into the penthouse.

All of these things were still true, but I also knew none of them were going to stop me. That's what made me the asshole in this whole situation. When given a choice, I inevitably made the wrong one.

But damn, did that woman look so *right*.

The French doors were open to the balcony, and she stood with one hip jutted out, a champagne flute in the opposite hand, looking at the city beneath us.

She was all graceful lines and fuckable curves, from the delicate slope of her shoulder to the neck I wanted to mark in some outdated, primal need to show the world that for one night, this woman found me worthy of her.

But the man who was actually worthy wouldn't take it.

I walked out onto the balcony, leaning back against the stone railing so I could look at the most beautiful view in the city. The lights, hills, and water of Seattle could never hold a candle to Paige.

"You came," she said, her voice shaking with the same fine tremor of her hand as she took a sip from her glass.

"Explain it to me."

"Explain what?" she asked, arching an eyebrow. "That I want you? Half the women in Seattle would admit to wanting you, and the other half are liars." Her gaze was steady, unwavering.

"You only want one night?" A soft breeze blew by, raising goosebumps on her bare arm. I removed my jacket and slipped it over her shoulders, which earned me a soft smile.

"Thank you."

"My pleasure," I said, loosening my bowtie so the ends hung down. "So about this one night?"

She cleared her throat and pulled the edges of my jacket closed. "Yes, I want a night. If that's amenable to you."

Amenable? One night spent with Paige under me? Who wouldn't be ecstatic over that?

"But—" she continued, cutting off my thoughts, "I also have a proposition that might benefit us both."

"You're literally propositioning me for sex? Isn't that illegal?" I teased.

A blush rose on her cheeks, and she looked away with a smile briefly. God, this woman wasn't just beautiful—she was captivating.

"Kind of," she admitted with a shrug. "You are in the middle of a PR nightmare."

I blinked. "We're really going to have to work on your pick-up lines." Of course she knew. Everyone in Seattle knew, let alone our closest friends.

"Well, there's no use beating around that bush. You are. I know you're up on contract, and that you're not exactly a PR asset to the Sharks right now. I could change that."

"How? By pretending to be my girlfriend like we're in some sappy rom-com?" One night, I could handle. But there was zero chance in hell I was faking anything in my life, let alone with a woman I honestly wanted.

Her shoulders straightened, and her chin rose a good

inch. Gone was the charming seductress—this was the savvy business woman. "Actually, I'm proposing that we enter into a real relationship with contractual limitations."

"I'm sorry?" I leaned in, certain I'd heard wrong.

"I have three months until I'm set to take over the company—until I sign a contract with a morality clause that puts an end to pretty much everything I could possibly want for myself. I'll basically be cloistered until an acceptable match comes along."

"So what you're saying is that until your Mr. Right comes along, you'd like me to be your Mr. Right-now?" Holy shit, could tonight get any weirder? *Here, have your dream woman for a while, but only because you're not good enough for her in the long-term.*

"No," she adamantly shook her head, those green eyes going wide. "I'm saying that I could improve your PR. I'm an upstanding member of the community. I sit on the board of several charities. I don't get drunk in public or do anything that would put me in the tabloids—"

"Yeah, you're a regular thoroughbred filly," I snapped, my insides twisting at the way she'd just laid out our differences.

She looked down, her shoulders sagging the slightest fraction, and I immediately regretted my words. But then she straightened, arched a delicate eyebrow at me, and my heart fucking lurched toward her, glad I'd said the words so I could have this moment.

"I am," she agreed. "And what I want is three months with you. A real relationship with a real end date."

"This doesn't feel a little Pretty Woman to you?"

"Not at all. It's a simple business transaction where we both benefit. We merge our lives for these three months, we both get what we need, we both get out unscathed and all the better for it."

"And what is it that you need?" I asked softly, stalking toward her. For every step I took, she retreated across the small balcony. She might act supremely confident, but the idea of proposing this insane little deal, and actually following through with it were two different things.

"To live." Her back hit the brick wall.

"Clarify," I ordered softly, running my thumb down the silk of her cheek. God, she was incredibly soft.

"I want to experience...lust. Passion. Everything I'm guaranteed to give up in three months."

My dick sprung, pushing uncomfortably against the fabric of my tux. "Why me?"

Her tongue slipped out, running along her bottom lip. "Because you're the only one I want, and I know that this would be the only chance I'd ever get to have you."

I studied the small shifts in her expression, the tiny nuances in her eyes that showed me her certainty, her determination, and the sliver of what I knew she wanted to keep hidden—her vulnerability.

"And when three months are up?"

"Your reputation is on the mend, and we both have contracts to sign and some great memories."

And when three months isn't enough?

I shoved that thought as far away as possible. This morning Paige was as untouchable as she was beautiful. She was a fantasy, like the first time a fourteen-year-old boy stumbled onto a Victoria's Secret catalog. Now she was standing in front of me, telling me I could have her for three months with no strings attached.

It was every man's dream. I'd be a fool to turn her down,

but I'd be an even bigger fool to walk into paradise only to know I'd be cast out in three month's time.

"Rory?"

"I'm thinking." I brushed back a loose strand of red hair. Could I have her for three months and walk away unscathed? Unlikely. She'd burn me to the very core, but damn if that wasn't a fire I was willing to walk through.

"I know it's an odd offer. And that you can have any woman you want in Seattle. Hell, probably the entire country. I'm not stupid. I see the magazines, the billboards, the thirty-foot tall poster of your face on the outside of the arena. And I know that I'm the one you'd be doing the favor for. I might not be a supermodel like that one girl last year—"

"There were two."

"—but. Wait, what? Two? I only knew about the one."

"I can be very discreet when the situation calls for it."

She blinked and took a steadying breath. "Right. Well, fine. Then I'm not like the girls you typically date, but I'm *good* for you—"

"Stop, Paige. Why are you trying so hard?"

A flash of uncertainty crossed her face; then I watched with amazement as all pretense of her shell crumbled. She sagged against the wall, leaning her cheek into my open hand. "Because I know you may need me, but I *want* you."

"That's where you're wrong. I want you, too. More than I've ever wanted any other woman."

I didn't wait for her response or her permission. Our mouths collided, opened for each other in the most carnal kiss I'd ever experienced. Her hands slid into my hair while mine gripped her hips, pulling her against me.

Damn, she fit against me like a dream.

Our tongues tangled, her taste all sugar and champagne,

better than any fantasy could have been. I instantly wanted more, harder, deeper, and I took it, giving her a clear vision of what things would be like between us.

I wasn't sweet and shy. I wasn't the fairytale prince who made love slowly. No, if that was what she wanted, she'd better know now before we agreed to...whatever this was. I took what I wanted, but I sure as hell made sure I gave back twice as much.

And right now I wanted Paige under me, her supple body reaching for mine, her thighs spread and quivering.

I gripped her ass in both hands and lifted her, groaning as her breasts rubbed against my chest.

"Wait, don't you want to see a draft of the agreement?"

"No," I growled, taking her mouth again.

I carried her into the massive suite, every ounce of my concentration torn between the feel of her tongue and not falling on my fucking face. I'd never had a woman strip every thought with nothing but a kiss. Never been so consumed that I seriously debated propping her up on the corner of that dining room table and taking her.

But I'd never had Paige in my arms.

Finding the bedroom, I set her on her feet and spun her in my arms, my fingers unerringly finding the zipper on the back of her dress.

"But there are terms, and I have this...well, bucket list of sexy things I'd like to—"

"Not tonight," I told her as her dress fell in a soft rush of silk to the ground. "While I'm more than intrigued by any sexy list you could think up with that insanely gorgeous brain of yours, tonight I just want my mouth on you."

"Oh," she said as I popped her strapless bra open. Her hands rushed up to hold it in place.

I inhaled her perfume, committing the moment to

memory. Then I gently tilted her head to the side and set my mouth to the side of her neck.

She sighed and leaned into me. "God, that feels good."

"Just wait," I promised, my voice thick with barely-leashed want.

"Does this mean you agree?" Her voice shook the slightest fraction.

I ran my hand up the flat, toned muscles of her stomach to twine my fingers with hers. "Think of this as an interview. If we both agree that there's something here, we'll consider a second round." Fingers locked, I pulled our hands away, and her bra fell to the floor.

She turned to face me, her eyes wide and luminous in the moonlight that filtered in through the windows. Stepping back, I looked down and sucked in a lungful of air. Her breasts were perfect with pink tips already drawn tight and waiting. Reaching out, I gently cupped one, reveling in its weight in my palm as she sighed.

"An interview," she whispered.

"Shall we begin?"

Yes or no. She may have said she wanted it, but I needed to hear it from her lips, needed to know this was really what she intended.

"Yes."

Sweetest word in the English language.

Cupping the back of her neck, I drew her into a kiss. She slid my jacket off my shoulders, and I let it fall to the floor with her dress before I picked her up by her tiny waist and laid her back on the king-sized bed.

I hovered over her, taking in every line of her body, learning with my eyes what I would explore and memorize with my hands, my lips, my tongue. She gripped my shirt and yanked, our mouths meeting in a frenzy of tongue and teeth. My dick strained against my pants, but there was zero chance in hell I was taking them off. I needed every barrier between us that I could get.

Breaking away from her mouth, I slipped kisses down her neck, across her collarbone, and down to her breasts. Her back arched and she let out the sweetest moan as I took one peak into my mouth, gently laving the crest with my tongue.

I'd been wrong before—yes wasn't the sweetest sound, that moan was.

"You taste like honey," I said as I moved to the other breast, willing myself to go slowly, not to blow it, both literally and figuratively. She was incredible, her skin softer than satin, and I stroked every inch her stomach, her breasts, her waist, until I reached the sweet flare of her hips. God, her curves would be the death of me.

Her legs moved restlessly as I placed hot kisses to the area her legs joined her hips, my tongue playing with the strap of her red lace thong.

"Rory," she pled.

I took a fortifying breath and tried to say the alphabet backward in my head as I pulled the scrap of fabric down her thighs, over her knees and slender calves until her panties joined the rest of her clothing and she was finally, gloriously naked.

If this was a dream, I never wanted to wake up.

"Now you," she said, raising up on her elbows.

"No," I answered, tasting the skin of her knee, then her thighs.

"But..."

I looked up and nearly abandoned my own plan. Damn, she was sexy, and beautiful, and classy, and everything that definitely shouldn't be in bed with a guy like me. "If this is going to work, we're going to have to agree to something, Paige. You might be in control in that boardroom of yours, but I'm in control in the bedroom."

"But I have a list—"

Without warning, I spread the lips of her pussy wide and ran my tongue from her entrance to her clit.

She gasped, her hands flying to my head. "Holy shit!" Her fingernails lightly scraped my scalp as she held me to her.

"See how much better it is when you stop thinking and start enjoying?"

I fucking loved her reactions, how honest they were. She wasn't some rehearsed model who wanted my paycheck and my last name. Paige just wanted *me*.

Circling her clit with my tongue, I waited until she ground her hips against my mouth and then rewarded her with just the right pressure, the rhythm that started her keening, whimpering my name.

"So fucking perfect," I groaned, soaking up every possible sensation of going down on Paige—her moans in my ear, her fingers in my hair, her taste bursting on my tongue. My cock was screaming, harder than it had ever been, but I'd never been more determined to keep it behind my zipper.

I licked, sucked, grazed my teeth across her, listening to her cries go higher, feeling her thighs tighten against my head, her breaths come quicker and quicker. It would be easy to get her off, a quick press of fingers just inside her, and she'd tumble right over. But I knew if I slipped my fingers inside her, my cock would be next, and that wasn't what tonight was about.

When she was writhing, pleading for release, I locked eyes with her. Then I replaced my tongue with my thumb, pressing on her clit exactly how she needed and slid down. I gave in to my primal need to know every inch of her, and instead of using my fingers, I fucked her with my tongue, sliding in and out of her tight pussy until she came, screaming my name.

I closed my eyes and put a tight leash on my dick. I was a grown man for fuck's sake, not a sixteen-year-old in the back of my dad's car.

Paige wanted control, wanted to set every rule, run every deal, and keep everything neat and tidy. That wasn't going to fly if she wanted me in her bed—in her life for the next three months.

I reared up over her and kissed her softly. "You are incredible, Paige. I could make you come for hours."

She blinked up at me, her eyes emerald green. "That...you...I can't...God, I can't even think."

"Good," I said, lightly kissing her nose.

It fucking killed me, but I slid off the bed, and retrieved my jacket from the ground, sliding my arms through the sleeves.

"Wait, we're not having sex?"

A smirk played at my lips. "Not tonight."

"You don't want..." her eyes dropped to the covers, and I immediately sat at the edge of the bed and pulled her into my lap.

I waited until she looked up at me, her cheeks still flushed from her orgasm. Then I kissed her, long and deep, knowing she could taste herself on my tongue. I didn't stop until she was as pliant as my dick was hard. Fuck, this woman tested me on every level possible.

"I want you," I assured her. "I would love nothing more than to strip out of these clothes and slide into you. Just thinking about it has my dick pulsing, Paige. I've never been this turned on just by getting a woman off, and I've never craved someone the way I do you. But this is interview round one, remember?"

I kissed her forehead and gently put her back on the bed. Then I stood and put as much distance between us as possible before I changed my damn mind. She was too tempting for her own good.

"When do we start round two?"

I smiled despite the epic case of blue balls that was currently threatening to unman me for the rest of my life. "Why don't you sleep on it, really make sure this is what you want."

"This is what I want!" she nodded enthusiastically. "And I can see that you want it, too."

I waited to speak until her eyes traveled back up my body.

"Well, I say that you need to wait. I'm not going to be a regret for you, Paige. I know you love control. You wouldn't be the business woman you are without it. But if you want *me*, then this is on my terms, not yours."

Her mouth dropped open, and I pressed my lips together to keep from laughing. It was going to be so much fun to rile her up over the next few months. I took a moment and let my eyes rake over her body from head to toe, savoring the delayed gratification because now that I knew how she tasted, how she sounded when she came, I knew we'd be explosive and worth the wait.

"Night, Red."

Her mouth was still open when I walked out of the hotel room.

I punched the button for the ballroom and thought about the least sexy things I could while the elevator made its descent. By the time the doors opened, my situation was far less dire and way less noticeable, but something told me I'd be sporting a semi until I had Paige again.

"There you are. Jesus, I've been looking for you all night," Mike, my agent, said, clapping me on the back and using his public smile as led me into a deserted hallway.

"I've been busy," I said.

He glanced at my undone tie and snorted. "Apparently. Anything I need to worry about?"

"Quite the opposite," I promised.

"Good, because I'm getting calls from the Sharks front office, and you are not on their bright and shiny list right now. You need to keep your nose clean and smelling like roses if you want any chance at renewing this contract."

"I always smell like roses," I said with a shrug.

"You smell like sex."

"Guilty." *Amazing, glorious sex.*

"For fuck's sake."

"Exactly," I laughed.

"Rory, I'm not fucking kidding. They've got your name on the chopping block, and they've made calls to Chicago to see if Armstrong would be up for a trade."

My stomach twisted. "Shit."

"Exactly," he repeated, mocking my earlier word. "Now take your ass home and figure out how the hell you're going to become the poster boy for Seattle Shark hockey before you lose your damned jersey."

I nodded, the severity of the situation hitting me like a sucker punch. I didn't say goodbye to any of the guys or acknowledge any of the women as I left the party.

Before, Paige's suggestion had seemed appealing for the sake of getting her in bed, and the off chance that I might be able to convince her I was worth more than three months.

Now it looked like I was going to have to agree not just

because I wanted her, but like she'd said—because I now *needed* her.

I'd never needed a woman, and I didn't intend to start now.

But I might not have a choice.

CHAPTER 4

PAIGE

MY BARISTA BROUGHT me another tall Americano and scooped away the empty mug I had sitting on my preferred table, nestled in the back corner of my favorite coffee shop.

"Thanks, Anne." I graciously took the steaming hot mug and inhaled the rich aroma before returning focus to my opened MacBook.

I didn't like going into the office on Saturday's if I could help it. I already clocked in seventy-hour work weeks, and I knew if I started making the "occasional" weekend visit, I'd end up living there. Still, I had the new financial reports for the end of the fiscal year to oversee, and I found the café an easy compromise when taking my work home with me.

My cell vibrated on the table, the screen lighting up with the one number I couldn't ignore.

"Hello, Father. Are you back in town?" I pressed the phone to my ear, scanning the empty tables surrounding me.

"Just landed an hour ago. George is driving me home. Your mother has a dinner party planned. Are you attending?"

"Not tonight. I'm still digging through the financial reports. By the time I'm done, my brain will be mush, and no match for Mom's guests." She always invited the most eclectic group of people—from intellectuals to hippies—and keeping up with the proper conversation eidetic quickly grew exhausting.

"You could pass them off to me and then *I'd* have the excuse." Dad chuckled.

"You've already been over them twice. You deserve the party anyway. I'm sure sorting out the east coast developments gave you one hell of a workload."

"True. I'm eager for the day I leave this all in your capable hands."

My heart raced, the excitement of finally running the company blooming in my chest. "Well, I'll be happy to take it off your plate."

"Speaking of plates, it seems you not only bought a seat at Matt Donaldson's event but enough for an entire table as well. Were you so taken with the cause?"

I sucked in a quick breath. It'd been a week since the night that ended too soon with Rory Jackson, but the memory was fresh and piping hot in my mind.

"I was," I replied, forcing all thoughts of Rory's expert tongue from my mind. *You're on the phone with your* father!

"Assisting those in developing countries to grow and maintain their water supply is essential for them to thrive," I continued hurriedly. "And Donaldson had more than done his due diligence with a well-prepared business model of how our donations would be used and the return it would give each location. Couldn't pass up the opportunity to be a part of it."

"You have your mother's heart and my brain," he said. "I'm sure he appreciated your donation, but the next time you want to drop three million in the cause, perhaps give your old man a heads up?"

I fought the urge to roll my eyes.

The money didn't make a dent in what my father had spread between numerous accounts. Being in the dark was what irked him. "Of course. I only didn't inform you because you were out of town. And besides, I made the donation in the company's name. It will be good for the cause *and* PR."

"Smart girl. Now, about that dress..."

I face palmed myself. Damn it. I'd thought Jennifer Laningston's fall outside the entrance of the Four Seasons would be enough to leave any shots the paparazzi had gotten of me in the trash. Father must've searched for it, or more likely he had my name on google alerts for whenever it hit the media. "It was a red carpet event—"

"Understood." His tone implied there was a silent *but* attached to the end of the response. *Cue lecture in three, two...*

"Paige," he said my name like I was fourteen again, asking to wear a halter top that had been all the rage back then. "You're about to be named CEO of the company that has given life-blood to our family for generations. It's successful because of what our family stands for. For our morals. We're a good, *wholesome* American family, and our public appearances have to show as much."

I'd heard the speech since I was old enough to pick out my own clothes and answer questions at press conferences. There was no need to re-lecture me on it. I was twenty-eight years old for God's sake.

"One question from the public on the purity of our lives could lead to questioning the purity of our products," he said, and I remained silent—as was expected of me. "Sales could drop. Thousands of our employees would be out of jobs. You know we take care of our own, and when you become C.E.O., it's not just about *your* needs anymore. It's your responsibility to ensure the stability of our employees' positions. Some of them have been with us for over thirty years. We can't be frivolous with our actions. We can't be impulsive..."

My father's voice tuned out as my mind shifted focus, hovering over the word impulsive and drawing up an image of Rory's deep blue eyes as they peered up at me from between my thighs. A warm shiver danced up my skin, teasing me with an intense ache I wanted soothed by only one man—a man who was the absolute *definition* of impulsive—and one who was a major risk I wasn't sure was worth taking.

"I only want what is best for you and the company," Father continued, and I blinked away the thoughts pulsing red in my mind. I took another sip of my Americano instead of stopping him. I knew—and had known—every stake of taking over our company for years now.

The bell on the coffee shop's door rang, and I about dropped the mug of hot coffee in my lap.

What in the absolute hell?

Rory Jackson walked up to the counter, a pair of dark blue jeans hugging his hips in all the right spots. A light gray t-shirt clung to his cut abs and chest, and the casual look was beyond sexy on him. Maybe even hotter than the tux and just shy of his Shark's jersey. *What is he doing here?*

I watched as Anne flustered behind the counter, taking his order and trying to control the giddy-school-girl grin on her face. I was instantly transported to that night, where he had touched me more intimately than anyone had before and yet he hadn't touched me near enough. The ache that had barely left returned with a vengeance as his smile lit up his eyes.

How could I have done that? Put out that offer, my fantasies, my *body*? My embarrassment was only topped by the relief that he hadn't taken everything I'd offered. *Relief, regret...whatever.* Not that it mattered. He obviously wasn't interested, and I wasn't chasing a guy who had to be convinced to sleep with me.

My breath caught in my throat, and I cleared it, remembering my father was still on the phone. "I'm sorry if I disappointed you. It won't happen again." I cut my father off mid-lecture, forcing my voice not to reveal the breathlessness caused by Rory's presence.

"I just need you to be aware of the incredible responsibility you're taking on in three months. It's not just the company's reputation at stake. It's our employee's livelihoods."

Good lord, it was just a dress! And it had worked. "I understand. Excuse me, father, but I have to go."

"Right. I'll see you on Monday. Unless I can convince you to change your mind about your mother's dinner party?"

"Too much work to do."

And one Shark to avoid like the plague he obviously thinks I am.

"Of course."

I hung up the phone and set it on the table, my eyes never leaving Rory's back. I know I'd had more scotch and sodas than I normally ever would've indulged in that night, but I remembered every single moment of his hands on my skin, his mouth on my core. I was *certain* I'd never told him about where I lived or where I liked to pass my time. This shop had been one of my best-kept secrets since I bought property a few blocks away over a year ago. And I'd never seen a Shark just *wander* in.

Anne giggled as she handed Rory a large, white paper cup. I quickly returned my eyes to the financial reports in front of me. Part of me hoped he'd walk out without seeing me, the other part—the lower portion of me that throbbed with a near painful pulse—begged to be seen.

"Paige?"

Oh good Lord, did he have to say my name like that? I couldn't hide the blush flushing my cheeks as I slowly brought my gaze up from the laptop.

"Rory."

He grabbed the chair opposite me with his free hand and dropped into it. His blue eyes sparked with a heat I recognized in my core, and the damn smirk he sported said he knew how much of an effect he had on me. I might as well be wearing a neon sign that said *Property of Rory.* "Good to see you."

I tried to return his smile. I'd crushed on the hockey star ever since he'd been drafted to the Sharks five years ago— how was it he'd rarely said more than two sentences to me all the times we'd seen each other at Bailey and Gage's, and now he acted like we were old friends? Seemed like the dirty-girl bucket list came with a set of karmic conditions— ones that made me face my own forwardness and the embarrassment over it.

Honestly, what had I been thinking making him a business proposition that included using him to check off every item I had on the list for the next three months? Of course, I knew it wouldn't hurt his reputation to be attached to me— the pristine Paige Turner—for three months, either, but still. I shouldn't have been so bold. I'd blame Jeannine, but I knew deep down why I did it.

Because you knew you would never get another chance like it even if you lived to be one-hundred. The reality of the fact had the fluttering butterflies dropping in my stomach like lead weights. I'd offered myself, and he'd decided the sample had been more than enough.

"They don't have coffee at the rink?" I asked, more upset with myself for wanting what I absolutely couldn't have.

"Ouch. Aren't you a tad bit happy to see me?" A crease formed between his eyebrows, the same one I'd glimpsed in the limo on the way to the Four Seasons last week. I sighed, my fingers twitching in my lap with the need to touch his face.

"I didn't mean—"

"It's all right." He waved me off, and the strained look was instantly replaced by the cool, confident face I was more used to seeing. "I'm not stalking you..." he arched a perfect eyebrow at me. "Unless that makes you hot?"

I sputtered around the sip of Americano I'd just taken, the joke cracking the wire-tight tension around the table that now seemed incredibly small with his form taking up the other half. "No, that doesn't do it for me."

He tilted his head, a few loose strands of blond hair falling on his forehead. He licked his lips, and I stopped breathing for a few seconds. He leaned back in his chair, smiling. "Bailey told me where you'd be."

Traitor. Best friend ever. Jury was still out.

"What can I do for you, Mr. Jackson?" I adopted the voice I used in the boardroom, knowing from our brief moments together he liked the idea of controlling a woman who was used to being in control.

"Careful, Red." He took a slow sip of his coffee. "Keep

talking to me like that and I won't be so careful with you in public."

My eyes widened. "Are you threatening me with PDA?" He cracked a grin, and I shook my head. "No, of course not," I continued. "Rory Jackson is a renowned playboy. Affection would be the last thing on his mind." The fact came out sharper than I'd intended and I parted my lips to apologize, but he held his hand up to stop me.

"You think you know me so well." He shook his head. "Read a few articles. Watch a few documentaries, and everyone is an expert on who I am and what I want."

I chuckled.

"What's so funny, Red?"

My heart raced every time he used his adopted nickname for me. I sucked in a breath, forcing myself to be as confident and calm as he was. "You forget I'm not just any fan."

"Oh? Are *you* the stalker now?"

"Hardly." I openly looked him up and down. "Though I do have eyes. And have been privy to your moves on more than one occasion while at Gage's."

"What are you talking about? I've never once tried anything with you there."

I sank back in my chair, suddenly giving too much thought to the reasoning behind that fact. "True," I said, ignoring the insecurities I had no point digging up. "But I was never the only woman there. In fact, I believe I've personally seen, and sometimes *heard*, you with five different women on five separate occasions." Not that I had counted.

He hissed, looking down at his cup and swirling the contents inside.

"Don't be ashamed," I said, reaching out and touching

his wrist. "I wouldn't be. I find it refreshing when someone can own who they really are and not give a shit who sees it."

He looked up at me, his eyes lighting up like he'd never seen me before. I pulled my hand back and grinned. "So," I continued. "No, I'm not the typical fan, but I do know you a little better than you think."

"Trust me. You wouldn't know what to do with me if you really knew me."

"I think I could handle it." I offered him my mug, and he tapped his cup against it. The silence was heavy as we took our drinks but not as awkward as I thought it would be.

"Now," I said, setting my mug down. "Tell me why you asked Bailey where I'd be today."

"Had a rough practice."

I arched an eyebrow at him. "And you thought I could help somehow?" *Did he want me to rub his sore muscles? While in the shower?* My mouth watered just picturing it.

He glanced around the café as if he feared we might be overheard. There were only a few other patrons in the shop, and they were across the room. The slow pace of the café was one of the reasons why I adored it so much. "Coach wouldn't let up on me. He's still pissed about the bar incident."

I nodded, completely understanding his coach's position. If one of my employees had as many violent encounters as Rory had, then I'd have the person on a three strike system. I gasped, tilting my head. "What strike are you on?"

A smile shaped his lips as he shook his head. "You never stop surprising me, Red."

"Not used to being with a woman with a mind of her own?"

"Am I *with* you? I thought we were just ticking items off a list, and I haven't seen a contract, yet." He licked his lips again, and I huffed, completely flustered every time the man brought any attention to his damn mouth—which I knew all too well what it was capable of doing to my body. "You have one, don't you? A contract?" He asked with a full-out grin. If I hadn't already been sitting down, my knees would have buckled.

"You're avoiding the question," I said, struggling to keep my composure.

"Which one?"

"Strikes."

"Ah," he said, sighing. "I've lost count."

My mouth popped into the shape of an O before I reigned it in. The idea of him being benched scared me almost as much as the idea of him taking me up on my offer of an exclusive relationship for three months. "You're the best enforcer we have. You can't keep this up, Rory. We need you."

He chuckled. "How long have you been a Shark?"

"Longer than you."

"Ha!" He smacked his hand on the table. "You're something else."

"I thought we established that the other night."

He leaned over the table, drawing closer to me. "We only scratched the surface that night."

My chest rose and fell rapidly as I couldn't hold a single breath with him so close, his scent tickling every nerve in my body. "Oh?"

He nodded, leaning back in his chair. "I'd like to take you up on your offer."

"*Oh?*" I wasn't capable of another word, the idea of having Rory to myself for three whole months before I had to swear off sex-God men like him forever stole every intelligible thought I may have had.

"Who could pass it up? You pitched it so well." His tongue ran across his lower lip like he could still taste me.

My thighs clenched.

"It's what I do."

"You ready for me to show you what *I* do?" He shifted his long legs beneath the table, his knee brushing mine. A flare of heat flew across my skin, and I glanced down at the financial reports I'd all but forgotten spread across the table.

"No," I said, my shoulder dropping. The crease between his brow was back, so I hurried on. "I have to finish this." I pointed to my laptop and stack of papers next to it. "How about dinner at my place tonight?"

He smoothed out his face in a blink and finished off the coffee in his cup. "Tell me when and where."

I clicked my pen and wrote out my address on a piece of paper. "I never give this out," I said, slipping it into his hand. "And if you could make sure the paparazzi aren't following you—at least until we finalize all the details of our arrangement—I would appreciate it."

He shook his head and stood, flashing me that brilliant smile that was equal parts charm and pure sex. Leaning down, he put his mouth right next to my ear. "You know, Paige, I think three months will give me just enough time to fuck that business tone right out of you."

Turning on his heels, he left me sitting there with my mouth hanging open with no words on my tongue. I watched him walk away, enjoying every inch of the view until he was out of sight. Fanning myself with one stack of reports that I had to get done, I shifted in my seat. Three months with Rory and I'd have to invest in an entirely new line of lingerie because I couldn't seem to keep dry around the man.

CHAPTER 5

RORY

FUCKING GROW a pair and go in already! My knee bounced uncontrollably in the back of the sedan, my driver waiting patiently as I sat and stewed outside Paige's house. I was already twenty minutes late—exactly the amount of time it had taken me to get to *Phantom,* walk inside the club and exit out the back entrance. The paparazzi had followed me and hopefully would wait there for me to leave through the front. Paige was clear on her terms when it came to the paps catching us before we knew exactly what we were doing.

Maybe that is why I couldn't get my ass out of the car. I'd never been nervous to have dinner with a woman. Hell, I didn't even twitch when a puck bunny had thrown me a curveball and showed up with my name tattooed on her hip.

No, I was a go-with-the-flow kind of man, but Paige was *all* business and *all* out of my league. When she made her offer, I thought I'd fallen into one of the many fantasies I'd had about her since the first time Bailey had introduced us. Three months of no-strings-attached sex with the redhead that invaded my dreams so many times I was waking up every day as hard as a teenager again? Hell. Fucking. Yes. And if it cleaned up my image enough to appease coach and keep me on the ice? Then win, win.

So why are you still sitting in the car like a scared little boy?

A deep breath and a mental kick in the balls later, I shoved open the door and told my driver I'd call him. He'd been with me for years and knew the score—sometimes I wanted a quick escape and others I didn't mind staying the night. I wasn't sure which tonight would turn into and always liked to be prepared either way.

I gripped the bottle of Merlot between fingers I refused to acknowledge were sweaty. I'd been with so many gorgeous women I couldn't count, why was Paige getting under my skin?

Because she's the first woman to see through your bullshit and the first one to ever go after what she wants with the same tenacity as you do on the ice.

Fuck, that was the truth. I'd *never* been with a woman like Paige, and for good reason. She was smarter than me, stronger than me, and had her whole life mapped out whereas I was simply trying to maintain some semblance of order in mine.

I wrapped my knuckles against her door, swallowing down the nerves that only flared in her presence. Gage would be furious the second he found out we were together —or whatever version of a story she wanted to tell people— but that shit I could handle. It was everything else I was worried about. What would being with a woman like Paige would do to me, even if it were only a few months? What happened if I couldn't hack it with her?

Or worse...if I fell for her?

The large mahogany door swung open, Paige leaning

against the knob in a smooth black dress that rested modestly below her knees but was tight enough to show off her impeccable body. My fingers itched to touch her smooth skin again and my mouth watered with the memory of her taste. She was fucking exquisite.

"I was beginning to think you'd bolt."

I stepped past her, handing her the bottle of wine. "What?"

She motioned to my driver who reversed onto the street. "You were out there for nearly ten minutes. You afraid I'd bite?"

I tilted my head. "How'd you—"

She closed the door and pointed to the corner of the ceiling behind me. A single camera pointed toward us, covering the entryway of the home.

"Ah," I said, turning back to her. "I see." My eyes trailed to her breasts, which peeked through the small V of her dress as she hugged the bottle of wine to her. I cleared my throat. "How many more of those do you have?"

She tapped her fingers against the glass bottle. "The whole house and exterior are covered." Her heels clicked against the hardwood floor as she moved through the entryway and I followed her into a dining room bigger than the one in my loft.

"Trouble with stalkers?" I joked as she set the bottle on the large wooden table that was set with two places. Candles illuminated the family style feast she had prepared —pasta and salad and fresh garlic bread.

She laughed as she darted into the kitchen that sat just off the dining room and returned with a wine opener. "I only have one stalker that I'm aware of," she said, eyeing me as she reached for the bottle.

"Let me." I stopped her, taking both items from her

hands and opening the wine. "Do you have a cook?" I asked, more because I wanted to know if we were alone in the huge house or if I had to watch my words around staff.

She shook her head, her soft red waves falling across her shoulders. "Of course not. Do you?"

I poured wine into the available glasses on the table and sat across from her. "No, I just didn't peg you for a woman who cooks."

"Ah," she said, wrapping her fingers around her glass and taking a slow sip. "Because I can't possibly run a company *and* be domestic?"

I pursed my lips, hissing. "Hit a nerve, did I?"

She licked her lips and set the glass down. "Maybe."

I raised my hands in defense. "Not intentional, Red." Her cheeks flushed the color of the wine, and I smirked. Every time I called her that she blushed. I made a mental note to do it as often as fucking possible.

"Moving on." She grabbed the wooden serving spoons and made me a plate. "I hope you like Italian." She handed it to me.

"I assumed as my biggest fan you would know it's my favorite." I cocked an eyebrow at her, wondering if we'd already started playing a game.

She laughed again, and my chest filled so much I couldn't breathe. I rubbed at the spot, squinting as I wondered about the source of the sensation.

"You all right?" she asked, setting her filled plate before her.

"Fine," I said and dropped my hand.

"Bailey told me."

"What?"

"Told me this was your favorite."

I grinned. "I've never been on this end of a seduction

before." I took a quick bite, and my eyes rolled back in my head. *Damn.* I might fucking marry her just to eat like this on the reg. I held up my finger. "Note, just because you made me dinner doesn't mean I'll put out."

Her fork clanked loudly against her plate as she swallowed her bite a little too hard, and my chest puffed out a fraction. I couldn't help it. I loved it when my mouth surprised her—in more ways than one.

"Well," she said, dabbing at her red lips with a napkin. "If I would've known that I probably wouldn't have put in all the effort."

"Ouch," I teased, taking another bite.

Her stunning green eyes stared at the wine in the glass before her lips a little too long.

"What is it?" I asked, the jokes suddenly drying up in my mouth.

She blinked a few times before taking a gulp. "Are we crazy?"

"*You* are. Without a doubt." I smirked. "Anyone who thinks they can put up with me for three entire months has to be."

She breathed out a sigh. "I think I can handle you."

"We'll see." I took another bite. "Where is your head at?"

"I..." she shook her head and reached for something in the seat next to her. "Here, it's easier to simply show you."

I took the folder from her hand, my fingers brushing hers and lighting up like an electric current buzzed between us. *Fuck, I might as well be a little girl in a fairytale.* The chemistry was unlike any I'd experienced before, and I couldn't fucking wait to see what would happen once I sank my dick inside her.

After months of fantasizing about it, and last week's

delicious sample, I was having a hard time keeping it in my pants. Especially since she was the one who wanted it so bad. But that was why I had to lock it up. She was used to getting her way. Used to being in control. And I wanted to offer her something she didn't have any experience in— being at the mercy of the man who wanted to worship her. That meant *I* called the shots on when I finally pushed her over the edge, and while I was beyond ready to take her there, it would be ten times better if I teased the hell out of her for a few weeks first.

My dick would hate me for it, but it'd be worth it.

I shifted the few pieces of paper inside, glancing over them. "I called it. You made a contract."

"No need to say I told you so," she said, taking another drink of wine.

"I know you better than you think I do." I cocked an eyebrow at her, glancing from the contract to her barely touched food and near empty wine glass. "Eat, Red. Wouldn't want you drunk for a business deal."

She grinned and picked up her fork, slowly taking a bite that drew attention to her perfect mouth. I'd never been more turned on watching a woman eat. I was so fucked.

After a few moments, she cleared her throat. "If there is anything not to your liking we can discuss amending it."

"Seems straight-forward enough," I said, closing the folder and setting it beside me on the table. "You have a list of items. I help you check them off. In return, you take me to charity events and parties and help me appear more *wholesome* to the public."

She nodded. "And..." she shifted in her seat, her clear nervousness over the discussion only making me want her more.

"Am I forgetting something?" I asked.

"You'll be exclusive...to *me* for the duration of the agreement."

A sting sliced at my chest and I resisted the urge to flinch. *What the fuck did you expect? She's seen you operate. Of course she'd think you'd fuck other women while you fucked her.*

I pushed back from the table, setting my napkin over my cleaned plate. Her eyes widened as I tugged on the wooden arms of her chair, easily forcing her to face me as I leaned over her. "You think being exclusive will be difficult for me?"

She swallowed roughly, her breasts rising and falling rapidly. My dick grew hard beneath my jeans, but I mentally told him to calm the fuck down. He wasn't running this show.

"Won't it be?"

I trailed my eyes up and down her body, tightening my grip on the armrests to keep my hands from slipping beneath her little black dress. "No, Red. Believe it or not, I've wanted you since I first saw you. Finally getting to taste you? That's worth the terms you've set."

She sucked in a breath. "And the fights? You can't do anything that reckless while we're together or it will ruin both of us."

I squinted at her, inhaling as I drew closer to her, taking in her sweet scent. "That will be harder."

"Impossible?"

"No. It can't be." Any more incidents and I'd be off the Sharks. That was the only life I knew—the only life I wanted—and couldn't lose it. I *wouldn't* lose it.

"Right," she said, her voice breathless. "Not only for the Sharks but for me as well."

"I read that part. I understand you have an image to

uphold." I shook my head. How the hell had this brilliant flame of a woman allowed herself to be contained in the space of a candle? All she needed was a little oxygen, and she'd burn brighter than any fire if she just gave herself the freedom to breathe.

"What?" She asked, her lips so close to mine it would only take a small tilt, and I could claim her mouth.

"No wonder you need me."

"We need each other," she corrected me, and the truth of the statement sucked the air out of my lungs. I froze above her, my eyes boring into hers. I didn't need anyone. Never had. This was completely new territory, and no one had exactly handed me a map.

"Whatever you say, Red." I brushed her lips with mine, just a breath of a touch but it was enough to turn my semi into a full hard-on.

"And," she said, licking her lips as I pulled back an inch. "Once the three months are complete we go our separate ways."

"Awh, you don't want to be friends?" I slowly slipped my knee between her legs, teasing her as I leaned closer, something in my chest rebelling at her imposed termination date.

She closed her eyes as I allowed myself to trail one fingertip down her bare arm. "We just can't fall in love." Her words froze my motions, and I reclaimed the armrest, gripping it so hard the wood creaked under the pressure. She laughed softly, opening her eyes. "That'll be the easiest part for you."

I pursed my lips, nodding. "Right." I wasn't a man who fell in love. I dropped panties. I changed women's lives with body shaking orgasms. Lust was my domain. Lust was all I was capable of. And the girl of my fantasies knew it. That's why she'd chosen me. So why did the notion make my chest ache—that I wasn't someone she could possibly see a long-term relationship with when I knew that was *exactly* the kind of girl she was. But that wasn't what she wanted from me, so maybe it was time to see exactly what she did. "Do I get to see this list?" I asked, suddenly needing to steer the conversation back to what I was good at—sex.

She shook her head, her eyes teasing.

"Really? How can help you if I don't know what needs to be done?"

She reached up, running her hands over my chest and down my abs. "I'll tell you when I'm ready."

I clucked my tongue at her. "What did I tell you about the control in this...whatever it is we're doing?"

"Relationship," she said. "Say it. Because that's what this is, and that's what everyone will believe. And where our relationship is going to be very open, the details of our arrangement have to be our secret."

I slid my tongue across her bottom lip. "*Relationship.*" The word might as well have been in a foreign language with how familiar I was with it.

"Good," she said and slipped her hand beneath the waistband of my jeans, her fingers reaching for what raged in my pants.

I hissed and pushed off the chair, putting a few feet of space between us. Her green eyes blazed as she looked at me in shock, and I smirked. "Tell me, am I just someone you chose to complete this list with, or am I *on* it?"

"Number seven," she answered instantly. She stood up, stalking toward me with the click of her heels echoing in my head. Damn, the fiery redhead would burn me from the inside out. I backed up until I hit the wall. "And I'm ready for that. Now."

She reached for me again, and I clasped my hands around her wrists pulling her toward me and spinning her until I pressed her back against the wall. Raising her arms above her head, I held her pinned there. "And who else is on this list of yours?"

"What?" Her eyes flew wide.

"This epic, dirty-girl list you have. If I'm #7, who else is on it?" The thought of tracking them all down and burying their bodies before they could touch Paige flew through my mind. *Way to go caveman.*

"No one. There's only you. I only want you."

I claimed her mouth. She tasted like wine and something a tad sweet, and it made my dick throb so hard I had to push against her.

Only me. I wasn't a nameless trophy fuck. I was the only one this insanely brilliant woman wanted, the only one she trusted with this list of hers, and I wanted her just as badly.

Gasping between my lips, she hooked her leg around my hip, shamelessly grinding against my dick as she sucked my tongue back into her mouth. "Fuck," I growled.

I had the woman pinned against the wall, and still she was taking control like no one else ever had. It would be so easy to sink into her—a quick unzip and slide her panties to the side, and she'd be screaming my name.

Holding her hands up with only one of mine, I trailed my free hand down her side until I felt the smooth skin of her bare leg, her dress hiking up to her hip. My fingers met black lace—and not fucking much of it—as I grabbed her ass and hefted her against me. Before she could hop to lock her ankles around my hips, I gently nudged her leg down. Stopping took the effort of a hundred two-a-day practices, but I kissed her one last time and backed away.

The creaminess of her skin was flushed, and her perfect breasts moved up and down as she caught her breath.

"Not tonight," I said.

She eyed the evidence of just how much I fucking wanted her. "Why?"

Because this is what you think you want, but it's not what you need.

I stepped closer to her, just enough to touch her chin. "I told you. *I'm* in control. I'll give you what you want, but only when you want it most."

"I want it—"

"No," I cut her off, smirking. "You think you do. Just wait." I winked at her and gave her a light kiss on her cheek. "Thanks for dinner," I whispered before returning to the table to grab the contract. "I'll sign this and bring it back." I tapped the folder as I opened her front door.

"When?" She asked, her hands popped onto her hips.

"Soon." She shut the door behind me as I stepped down her porch and walked slowly to her driveway.

As I waited the ten minutes for my driver to pick me up, I battled the urge to say, "fuck it," bust back through her door and carry Paige to her bed and sink deep inside her like my body begged.

She wasn't a woman you fucked quickly to get out of your system. She was the kind you savored. The slow burn that only made the flames brighter the longer you stoked it. Paige was a living, breathing flame. I just hoped I was strong enough to withstand her fire.

CHAPTER 6

PAIGE

MONDAY MORNING and I was a tension-riddled mess behind my desk. It'd only been two days since dinner with Rory and his more than successful tease. I craved him like a glass of ice water on a hot day. His skin, his scent, his touch, were all I could think about. Which definitely didn't help me focus as I finalized the details on an employee appreciation event for a thousand staff members from different departments in the company.

The event was a bi-annual occasion we held in order to keep up morale as well as give employees the chance to voice any concerns or ideas they had for the future of the company. It was a tradition, and one I looked forward to each time. Still, if I wasn't careful, I'd be scheduling the event at the Shark's home rink with no more entertainment than to watch Rory shred the ice during practice.

A buzz rang from the intercom on my desk. I clicked the button. "Yes?"

"Mr. Turner is here to see you."

"Send him in." I clicked off the com and smoothed my hair down while slipping my bare feet into my black pumps.

I didn't have any meetings today and had gotten comfortable while approving the event coordinator's band choice for the appreciation party this weekend. *Comfortable* wasn't a word my father understood.

The wooden doors to my office swung open—my father was never one to make a subtle entrance. He wore one of his traditional gray, pinstriped suits that brought out the silver in his hair.

"Paige." He opened his arms as I came around my desk.

"Father." I hugged him, genuinely happy to see him. I always missed him when he went out of town on business, which often kept him away for weeks at a time, even when I was a child. I'd gotten used to seeing him around the office, where we would have daily lunches if meetings and schedules allowed it, and once he retired...well, I guess I'd have to grow up after all.

"You look lovely," he said, pushing me out and glancing at my three-piece black pant-suit and blazer combo.

"Thank you." I didn't miss the emphasis in his compliment or the silent *this is what the CEO of our company should present herself as* part of the sentence. It didn't bother me, as long as he was done lecturing me about the damn red dress. It had gotten me into more trouble than I knew how to handle—though it was also responsible, at least in part, for snagging me Rory for the next three months, too.

"Everything set for this weekend?" He took a seat in one of the leather chairs I kept in front of my desk.

"Yes." I sat back down in my chair, clicking a tab on my computer. "Jeannine says she has something special planned for the self-serve stations." I chuckled at my father's panicked look. Our designated go-to caterer, and my best friend since sixth grade was one of the best chefs in the country—it was her wild lifestyle that had always concerned him. Started with the night she'd snuck me my first shot of Jack Daniels freshman year in high school. Father had flipped, forbidding our friendship, but my mother had talked him down.

"You know she'll take care of everyone." I shifted my full focus on him. "And this year I've made a few changes."

"Oh yes?"

I nodded. "We always stock enough food and drink to feed two times the number of guests, and since we always offer a casual yet classy atmosphere, one where patrons can pick and choose from the courses, I'd like to invite the frequenters of one of the local shelters to dine after our guests have served themselves."

He pinched the bridge of his nose.

"We threw out so much food last time. It's a waste of our resources."

"And this has nothing to do with your pet project?" He smiled and tilted his head.

He knew all about my ambitions and how I'd use them to not only keep our company profitable but expand into other areas as well. "Seattle has a need. We can fill it. At least for one day, we can make a dent in those who go hungry on a daily basis."

"Have you considered the consequences if the new names on the guest list don't mingle well with the employees and stockholders the event is for? Or perhaps if the stockholders don't take kindly to their presence?"

A sour taste filled my mouth. Of course, I'd thought about the scenario, but I had enough faith in humanity to push forward. Didn't mean I hadn't done my due diligence, though. "I've doubled security in case there are any confrontations. But there won't be. Our name, our *brand* is about providing the highest quality products and best service to the people who need them. These people *need* to eat. We'll have an influx of food that day. It makes sense."

He rubbed the five o'clock shadow surfacing on his chin. "Your heart never ceases to surprise me. Nor does the tenacity in getting what you want." He stood and came around the desk to kiss me on the forehead. "Make all the arrangements. I'll sign off on whatever you need."

My heart lifted at the idea of all the people who would get to experience a five-star meal and eat their fill. "Thank you."

He glanced around my desk as if a company check would pop up that needed his signature.

"I already approved it. The three most overcrowded shelters were contacted this morning."

He chuckled. "Of course. What need of me do you have anymore?"

"Father..."

He shook his head, reigning in his laugh. "You're my perfect successor. I have no doubt."

He kissed my head again before leaving, and I slumped back into my chair. Usually, the pride I garnered from making my father proud was something I relished. Today, I couldn't help but feel it was unmerited.

After all, I'd already crossed off several numbers on my dirty-girl bucket list—#9: *Purchase my first sexual paraphernalia* (a scary looking red vibrator that, in fact, Jeannine had bought on my behalf so there would be no paper trail) and #3: *Watch a M/M porn film* (another endeavor Jeannine had been all too happy to join me in. Bailey had been there too, with popcorn and wine and many, many heated breaths)—and I couldn't stop seeing the circle drawn around #7. It would be completed soon, along with the rest of the list unless Rory changed his mind and didn't sign the contract.

Number seven teased me with urgency, and yet it was easily the most damning on the list.

How could I be the face of the corporation I loved when all I wanted to be was Rory's?

———

"A week and a half and you don't call or respond to any of my texts—what makes you think you can waltz in here and demand a drink?" Jeannine's snark didn't match her smile as I took a seat at the large, wooden bar.

"Drink *and* a meal, let's not forget that."

She shook her head, her normally wild blonde curls tucked into a ponytail. She ran her hands down her immaculate white chef's jacket. "Depends. Are you willing to sing for your supper?"

"Absolutely,"—I leaned over the bar, lowering my voice so only we could hear—"and *boy* do I have a song to sing. After a scotch and soda."

"Tease." She laughed but immediately poured my favorite drink and slid it in front of me.   I unbuttoned my blazer and stretched my arms over my head, rolling my neck in an attempt to ease the tension there. It didn't work—hadn't worked the past few days. I'd come to the conclusion I'd never fully relax again until Rory picked up where he left off at my place. The image of him pinning me against the wall in my dining room flashed red hot in my mind, as it had so many times since he'd left me there to take an extremely cold shower. Had to give the man credit, though. He knew how to make me ache in places I never had before.

I glanced around Jeannine's restaurant—one of three

she owned—my eyes hunting for anyone who might take an interest in my anticipated gossip session with my best friend.

The place was slow since it was well past ten p.m., and only a few patrons nursed glasses of red in a booth nestled in the far back corner. *Nine's* was a Michelin star winner, and one of the only places Jeannine played head chef at on a regular basis. It was a sweet perk, never needing a reservation in order to get the highly sought after food but she'd been cooking for me since our "family studies" course in middle school.

"You milk that while I throw together your usual." She nodded toward my drink and disappeared into the kitchen in the back.

I took a sweet sip, enjoying the immediate release I received from the smooth scotch. Well, at least that was something. I closed my eyes, unable to keep the image of Rory from my mind. I'd had a few lovers—discreetly—since college, and I couldn't understand what it was about Rory that tangled me so badly, especially since we hadn't even officially had sex yet.

Maybe it's because he's taking control over you in a way no else ever has before.

Another sip. I'd never once wanted a man as badly as I did Rory—and I knew it had less to do with his celebrity-athlete status and more to do with the way he took control of the situation, of *me*, despite my efforts to take the reins. I may have drafted the contract, but he was the one with all the power. The push-pull, paired with how little I truly knew of the man, made it so much more intense.

"Lobster risotto," Jeannine said as she slid the plate before me, "with a side of *you better tell me what the hell went down in the penthouse.*"

I smirked, picking up my fork and slowly taking a bite. My eyes rolled back in my head. Jeannine had a direct line to my soul and had found the easiest route through food. The dish practically melted in my mouth. "Perfection. Every. Time."

"Yes, yes. The deets. Now." She leaned her elbows on the bar, giving me her undivided attention. Of course, she'd practically made the dirty-girl bucket list for me and made sure I was under strict orders to share every situation which resulted in checking the items off.

"He came up a few minutes after you handed him the key."

She clapped her hands together, drawing the attention of the diners in the back. I eyed her, and she threw her hands up in apology. "Sorry. I knew he would. Who could resist you?"

"Oh, please." I rolled my eyes.

"So what happened?"

I sighed, thinking about how close he'd taken me to the edge before pulling me back. "We're taking it slow."

Her shoulders dropped. "Slow? Who has time for slow?"

Heat flushed my cheeks as the memory of his tongue between my thighs ignited the ache that flared every time I thought about him. I shifted in my seat, leaning further over my risotto.

"So are you dating? I thought he didn't do that." She tilted her head.

I shrugged. "I think we are."

She squinted at me. "You're serious?"

"Why not?"

"Because he's Rory Jackson."

"And I'm Paige Turner. So what?"

"You know his reputation. I was all for you using him for a little list checking, but a relationship? Is that...smart for you?"

Guilt twisted my insides. There wasn't a time in my life I'd ever lied to Jeannine. Or Bailey for that matter. Now, with the deal I'd struck with Rory, we'd be lying to everyone —kind of. It was complicated. I couldn't risk them knowing, though. It wouldn't make sense to them, and it definitely wouldn't be good if word got around I practically hired one of Seattle's hottest Sharks to be my sex slave. *Ugh. When you put it that way...*

I reached across the bar and squeezed her wrist. "I love you for looking out for me, but you know I'm a smart girl. I don't go into any situation blind, and I know exactly what to expect when it comes to Rory Jackson. I've been given a first class seat to his many...one night relationships. I won't get hurt."

She eyed me skeptically, almost as if she could see through my line of bullshit. I wouldn't doubt her the ability, but I was thankful she didn't press the issue.

"All right," she said, finally, her light smile returning to her face. "Did he talk about his stick and Shark stats all night?"

I chuckled. "No. We didn't actually talk...much."

She arched an eyebrow. "You dirty girl!"

I couldn't help but join her laughter. Lord, we could've been in high school again. Only now the men we discussed were more than capable, incredibly hot, prospects. "I know! I'm terrible!"

"No, you're not." She fiddled with the collar of her jacket. "You went after what you wanted. Always have. I love that about you. I wish I had half your courage."

"Please, I wouldn't have made the list without you pushing it. And look at the success you have!"

"I don't have an evening with Rory Jackson under my belt!"

"I don't either." I shoved another quick bite into my mouth. "Not technically."

"At least tell me he's a good kisser," she begged.

The memory of his mouth was imprinted on my soul, his tongue was that magical. "Yes. In fact, I've never had better."

"Shut up!" she giggled. "Damn. Think about how good it'll be when you finally sleep with him.

A warm shiver shook my core. "I have."

"Unless it's all build and no backing it up."

My fork clinked against the plate. "Thanks for being a Debbie Downer." I shook my head. "Besides," I leaned forward, lowering my voice to a whisper. "There is no possible way he could be bad. I practically soak my panties every time the man walks into the room."

She hissed, fanning herself as I returned to my meal. "Wait. You've seen him since Donaldson's event?"

"Twice." I grinned. "I ran into him at Aroma's and then invited him over for dinner later that night."

"You *are* so bad!"

I nodded. "He actually *found* me there."

"Like, sought you out?"

"Mmmhmm," I mumbled around another forkful. "Got the info from Bailey. Not that it took much, I bet. The two of you would probably make him a key and give him my security code if he asked for it."

She laughed. "Can you blame us? Look at you! You're blushing just talking about him, and that smile on your face has to hurt because you've been wearing it since I brought him up!"

I touched my cheeks, forcing myself to drop the school-girl grin.

"Pulling the Bailey card is smart. Seeking you out and now *dating*?" She rubbed her hands together. "He fell for you quick. That's a record. Way faster than Kevin. What it'd take him, three weeks?"

"Stop it. Kevin was in high school...but yes, he dropped the L-bomb after only three weeks."

Not that Rory would ever use that word.

"When are you seeing him next?"

"I don't know, the next high school reunion?"

She planted me with a firm gaze that told me she wasn't talking about Kevin.

"I'm not exactly sure."

"Why the hell not?"

"He said he'd call."

She sighed and took a good swig of my scotch. "Well, I sure as hell hope he does quick. You have to indulge while you can, and we didn't set any repeating clauses on the dirty-girl list. You could check off number seven until you can barely walk."

I swallowed my bite a little too quickly. "Jesus, Jeannine!"

"Seriously. No one would ever know."

I dabbed my lips with a napkin. "Because gossip surrounding the bad boys of the Sharks never makes head-lines? Please. That's why we're taking it slow. So the media sees we're both serious about..." I let my sentence hang there, my imagination running wild with every way the media could destroy my name and that of the company I was meant to head.

"I get that," she said. "It's just..."

"What?" I asked after she'd held her breath for a few moments.

"You've always been in control, constantly maintained the good-girl image your family—and now your position—has demanded of you. It'd be nice to see you let someone else take care of *you* for a change. I hope whatever you two are doing at least accomplishes that."

I pressed my lips together. She was right, as usual. This is why she was my soul-sister. She knew *me* better than me sometimes. Of course, Rory had gotten under my skin so deliciously—because he'd taken full control and left me wanting more.

"Did you at least sneak a photo with your phone?" Jeannine brought me out of my wild thoughts—where *I* hunted Rory down and forced him to finish the delicious game he'd started.

"Of course not. If you want to know what he looks like without a shirt, google it. It's very close to the real thing...except..."

"What?"

The image of the deep V that the cotton towel had barely covered when I'd seen him at Bailey's made my mouth water. "He's well defined in ways Photoshop could never touch."

I chuckled at her wide, opened mouth, watching as the gears turned behind her eyes. She snapped out of it, and lightly smacked me on the shoulder. "And you want to take it slow? You're insane."

"We have to." It didn't matter that I wanted to test the limits Rory would push me to or the rules he'd make me break. "There is too much at stake if we push it too fast. Not just my name, or his reputation, but my employees. They're the ones who would suffer the most if our company got dragged through the gutter with too many *immoral* head-lines associated with my name. And we all know the kind of stories the press writes about him. He needs the slow pace as much as I do."

She hissed. "God it's like your family are a bunch of politicians."

Close, at least with the moral standard the world held us to. I couldn't be mad about the life I'd grown up in, though. I believed in those morals, believed I was a good person...I just wanted to do a few bad things before I shut the door on that kind of life forever.

Twelve bad things to be exact.

And, damn it, the only one that kept my breath catching and heart racing was number seven. If Rory didn't put me out of my misery soon, I might combust before he had the chance.

Jeannine reached across the table and clutched my wrist. "Even politicians make it work. I'm not saying he's prince charming and will change overnight, but I get you wanting to see where it goes between the two of you. I see how flustered you are simply talking about him. I can't imagine what he does to you in person."

Warmth filled my insides, and I licked my lips.

"Or maybe I can." She let go and laughed as she took my nearly cleaned plate back to the kitchen.

I loved her support, even when she knew the stakes as well as myself. Again, I had the urge to tell her the truth, tell her that Rory and I had nothing more than a business arrangement, but that was one secret I couldn't risk anyone ever finding out.

Gorgeous rays of Seattle sun illuminated the botanical gardens I had secured for the employee appreciation event, making the rich array of colorful flowers pop against the lush greenery. Round tables draped in the standard cream linens took up the area used for entertainment, and Jeannine had set her team and self-serve stations to the right of the stage I'd had constructed on the site. It acted as the focal point of the event, and the indie-band I'd hired—Black Orchid—were two songs in.

I stood near the entrance beneath an archway of ivy and greeted our guests as they came. Almost everyone had arrived, from our stockholders to the people who ran our packaging department, and the line for food dwindled as our employees filled their plates with signature Jeannine dishes like my favorite lobster risotto, seared scallops, and pan-seared halibut. She was busy busting her moves behind the stations, practically dancing at the ovens placed back to back, allowing her to maintain the supply as soon as it came close to a shortage.

"Paige." My father's voice drew my attention back to the entrance, and I smiled as he wrapped me in a side hug. "This is gorgeous. Well done."

I scanned the area another time, noting the vast amount of empty tables waiting to be filled resting toward the back, and nodded. "Thank you. Our other guests should arrive any minute."

"Wonderful. The musicians have talent, and I'm glad they're sticking to melodies that please a wide span of tastes —I can't tell if they're folk, modern, or blues."

"Indie. An eclectic combination of several genres. It's why I picked them, their wide appeal."

"You are an extremely smart woman, providing the best for our employees, and inviting those in need to dine as well. Honestly, I couldn't have thought of a better way to represent our company and the wholesome name behind it."

I pressed my lips together, accepting his words as a compliment, but knowing I hadn't once thought about the benefits of inviting the shelter guests for our company. I genuinely wanted to help. I couldn't care less if the news or top-bloggers picked it up or not, though I wouldn't put it past my father to have called and scheduled their arrival regardless. He couldn't help it; it was the businessman in him.

"How did you manage to snag so many wonderful items for the charity auction?" He eyed the station to the left of Jeannine's set-up, a long rectangular, cloth-draped table holding the items he spoke of.

I shrugged. "I learned from the best."

A prideful grin shaped his mouth. "You sent Kelsey after them?"

I chuckled. The petite brunette, currently inhaling a plateful of scallops at one of the center tables had been my personal assistant for six years. She'd applied for the position just to earn some money while she completed her masters in art history, but it was her minor in public relations that had won me over. That and her ability to find the humor in even the stuffiest of business situations. Her ability to discover local artists—from painters to musicians to writers—and bend them into donating items was the ultimate bonus.

"How did she manage to obtain Rory Jackson for the day?"

My head snapped to my father, eyes wide. "Excuse me?"

"Were you unaware? He's already given a considerable

check and donated a set of signed hockey sticks. I haven't a clue why anyone would want them, beat up and used as they are, but the bid is already in the five figures. I believe one of our shareholders has the same crush you do."

Of course, father wouldn't understand why anyone would want to get their hands on Rory's stick—he didn't keep up with sports, let alone the NHL. I nearly choked over the word *crush* picturing all the not-so-innocent *crush-like* things we would be doing to each other over the next three months...I *hoped*. This time when I gazed over the crowd, I hunted for one face.

"Looks like he's getting acquainted with Jeannine." Dad pointed toward her station where she'd amazingly left her position at the ovens and served him herself. I didn't bother explaining to my father that we were all already acquainted.

Instead, I smoothed my hands over my white day dress, resisting the urge to cinch tighter the red ribbon that circled my hips. "Excuse me, father." I patted his shoulder before walking over with what I hoped was a super casual and not at all shocked look on my face. I knew I'd see him again, but at my company's bi-annual appreciation event was the last place I had expected it to happen.

Jeannine waggled her eyebrows once we locked gazes and Rory, noticing her shift from bright-eyed-smile to crazy-innuendo face, glanced my way.

I stopped a foot away from him, my breath stalling in my lungs. The man looked good in everything, his black slacks and royal blue polo beyond making his eyes pop. He could wear a prison jumpsuit, and he'd drip sex. I clenched my eyes shut for a moment, forcing the images of what laid beneath the clothes from my mind.

"What are you doing here?" I wasn't breathless. I was... upset. Fantasizing about sneaking around with him was one thing, having him show up at a corporate event—without so much as a heads up—was an entirely different situation. Especially with my father's watchful eyes measuring each step of my success and each of his prayers for me not to fail him—even more so with the new addition to the guest list that would be here any second. I know the contract stated we'd be a couple, but I'd wanted to inform my father of my new "relationship" on my own terms, not Rory's. Though, the man was constantly reminding me who was in control now that I'd enlisted his help.

"Couldn't pass up an opportunity to give back to the local community. Wonderful charity you chose for the event, Paige. So many homeless shelters will benefit from the boost in funds."

My heart actually had the gall to flutter in my chest. *No.* I slapped the bitch down and redirected the feelings to my pussy where they belonged. Sex was acceptable. Lust was fine...actually having feelings for him would make our arrangement even more dangerous than it already was.

"Thank you, Rory." I was shocked he'd shown up—him looking into the charity event was beyond my thought process. He wasn't advertised in the media as a do-gooder, but he'd already came to my aide at two charity functions. I'd always thought it was on Bailey and Gage's insistence, but perhaps there was a side to him no one knew. The media constantly focused on which model was on his arm this week, or what player on the opposing team he'd crush next. This—what he was doing with me or for me or whoever the hell knew—would be fantastic for his image. And he'd be fantastic for my...list. *No butterflies, Paige. Just business.*

I eyed Jeannine. She was easily the most gorgeous person here—besides perhaps Rory—even with her platinum blonde locks tied up in a top-knot and her all black chef attire.

She suggestively wiggled her hips while Rory's attention was on me and I chuckled. She'd be a better match for him than me, easily able to keep up with his wild side, and she didn't have anything at stake from being in the limelight. Hell, her restaurants were frequented by A-listers all the time. She was used to it.

A pang of completely unmerited jealousy cut in my stomach. When the hell had I decided I'd rather not picture Rory with anyone else? He was only mine for three months. After that, it would be back to bed-hopping for him and near-celibate for me.

"Well, this looks divine, Jeannine. Thank you." Rory licked his lips as his eyes trailed my body before he held up his full plate and sauntered to an empty table near the auction items.

Jeannine whistled. "He just eye-fucked you in public, girl. I told you he's got it bad."

I darted my gaze left and right, thankful no one was near enough to catch her words. "No, he doesn't." And the mere thought did *not* make my heart beat harder. Nope. It was just the way his ass looked in those slacks as he'd walked away.

My second guest list made the perfect timing to arrive, and I hurried over to the entrance to greet them. "Thank you all for coming," I said and pointed to Jeannine's stations. "Please feel free to fill your plates, sit where you'd like, and enjoy the entertainment. After you've had enough to your liking, please stop by the auction table and pick up your raffle ticket. We'll be holding a drawing after the auction."

I received several hugs, a few handshakes, and plenty of skeptical looks as people who varied in age and sex pushed on to the food, creating a fast but well-formed line. After satisfying myself that everything was running smoothly, and with the band in full swing, eliciting some people to dance before the stage, I made my way over to Rory.

He grinned over his empty plate, the look all too confident that he'd known, without any doubt, *I'd* come to *him*.

I took a seat next to him, adjusting my dress over my legs underneath the cloth that draped over the table.

"You know, we joke about the stalking thing, but it isn't *really* sexy. That junk only exists in the movies."

He placed a large palm over his chest. "You wound me."

"Please." I laughed.

Shifting in his seat, he angled his legs toward me under the table, his knee brushing mine. "I have some paperwork for you in my car. Signed. Aren't you excited, *honey*?"

The way he said the pet name was forced and awkward enough to make me laugh. Nothing like the real nickname he had for me, which made me shiver whenever he dropped it. "I'm thrilled, darling." I teased him. "I can't imagine how terrible this will be for you," I said, lowering my voice.

"Fun." He shook his head. "It'll be fun. You can at least admit that."

The ache between my thighs had yet to be satisfied, so I shrugged. "Still waiting to see."

He leaned to whisper in my ear. "Admit it. You got wet the second you saw me."

My lips parted, and I swear I didn't mean to gasp. I glanced around with panicked eyes, as if anyone could've heard his hushed tone. My confident and controlling persona was useless here, surrounded by all the people whose livelihoods depended on our profitable and well-functioning company.

His fingers grazed the bare skin of my thigh, pushing

underneath the skirt of my dress, and rising dangerously high. Blood pumped so hard through my veins it rushed in my ears.

"Wow. I've never seen you speechless, Red." He stopped his ascent but kept his hand on my leg. Just two inches to the right and he'd be able to touch me where I ached.

I didn't dare move, unable to deny the pulse-pounding adrenaline I received from his direct advance in a very public place—not that anyone could see—the draped cloth covering everything that mattered.

I locked eyes with him. "You haven't known me that long."

"Something I'm trying to remedy. We've only got three months. Have to make it count."

"Look who is taking his duties more than a step farther."

"What makes you say that?" He took up his massaging of my thigh again, and I swallowed hard, my mouth suddenly dry.

"It seems like you're taking an interest in my personal life. What *matters* to me. That's dangerously close to ruining the casual agreement we've struck." I intertwined my fingers on the table top, fearing if I let them wander they'd plunge down his pants. *Good Lord I couldn't keep it together around this man.*

He smirked. "Casual?" He eyed me. "Come on, Paige. You and I both know nothing between us has been casual."

"I'm proud, though. Your donations and presence here today will help jumpstart that...*wholesome* image we're going for." I tried to reference the business side of our deal in order to cool the fire pulsing between my thighs, but my words still came out stuttered with each movement of his hand on my skin.

"You know what I've told you when you go all board-room on me?" He shifted closer to me, slowly tugging one of my hands underneath the table to lightly graze the outline of his extremely hard cock. "Keep talking like that, and I'll forget I'm playing the good boyfriend who holds hands and does brunch."

His words soaked my panties, and I wiggled in my seat. Damn it, he had a direct line to my *fuck me now* button— one I hadn't known existed until I'd met him.

"Rory I—"

"Saying my name only makes it worse, Red." He hissed, and his fingers found my wetness under the table with no pretenses of light petting. He dove right in, pushing my panties to the side and stroking my clit with an expertise that had me immediately in sparking knots.

I sucked in a deep breath, unable to tear my eyes away from all the potential people who could catch us. They danced, ate second portions, or browsed the auction table, not ten feet from where we sat—and they were all *thankfully* oblivious.

My body? Not so much.

Rory kept his eyes on me, grazing over my chest, which I tried beyond belief to keep control of. The act was harder than anything I'd ever done, and I was a fucking Harvard graduate. Sparks shot across every surface of my skin, the heat from his touch burrowing deeper in my core as he slipped his fingers inside me.

God, why did I have to wear a dress?

He pressed his thumb against my clit as he pushed his fingers in deeper.

Scratch that. Thank God I'd worn a dress.

My breath quickened, and I couldn't help it, I moved against him with the smallest of motions, silently begging him to make me come...regardless of the people surrounding us. I'd needed the release at his doing since the first night in the penthouse. He'd kept it from me for so long I was ready to jump him at my own company's event! I wiggled again, imagining his strong hand was the strong cock I knew he had.

He jolted, immediately withdrawing his hand. He pushed back from the table, waving to the crowd who I only just now realized had their eyes on him.

"Thank you," he said after he'd climbed on stage and the crowd had started applauding. He silenced them with one raise of his hand. The same hand that had been *inside* me seconds ago. *Holy hell.* "I promised Paige I would say a few words. Promised her they'd be clever. Well, I'm going to have to break my promise as I've misplaced *that* priceless speech."

Everyone laughed, but I remained lost in my head, in the heat still throbbing between my thighs. *How could I lose it like that? How could I let him do that to me with the chance of getting caught so very close?*

"What I will say is thank you all for coming. For contributing to a corporation that has helped keep families healthy and *wholesome* for decades." The way he emphasized the word *wholesome* had me grinning despite the insane terror mixed with need rushing in my blood. It was like he was speaking only to me, not the hundreds in the crowd. "You're all wonderful people that I'm honored to have met today," he finished, flashing that million-dollar smile and descending the stage to another round of applause. He even stopped to snap quick photos with anyone who asked.

I thought the separation would be like a cold shower and shock some sense into me.

It didn't. He only turned me on more, showing a side I'd never seen before—at least a side the media had never shown coverage on. His eyes caught mine across the crowd and I didn't miss the lust that flashed behind them.

I crossed my legs, unable to ignore the slickness between the motion.

The auction winners were announced and collected their items right after his speech, and then, per my direction, Kelsey had drawn a numbered ticket from the raffle I'd had the shelter guests collect from. The winner had two children with her and hugged them before rushing up to meet Kelsey. She didn't know she'd just won a check big enough to feed her family for a year; she was just happy to win anything at all. It broke my heart and made me fill with pride at the same time.

And just as I was mentally plotting all the people I could help once I took over as C.E.O., Rory drew my attention and motioned toward the parking area just outside the gardens. I quickly followed him to his car secretly hoping he'd throw me in the passenger seat and take me to his place for an entire night of nothing but him and a set of sheets.

Instead, he opened the door and pulled out the same folder I'd given him over dinner. "It's official." He handed me the contract which I glanced at. It was signed. "You're mine for three months."

The claim sent another wave of heat across my skin. I straightened, arching an eyebrow at him. "I believe this states you're *mine*, Mr. Jackson. Do we need to go over the articles again?"

His hands snaked around my hips, the movement innocent, but it was enough of a public display that if anyone were watching they would know we were "together."

"Only if you want to give me an actual peek at the list, Ms. Turner."

I chuckled, shaking my head and moving his hands from my hips, keeping hold of one with my hand. "Why are you so interested in the list?"

"Why wouldn't I be? If *I'm* number seven, I can't imagine what else made it on there."

I playfully smacked his chest. "Overconfident much?"

He squeezed my hand. "Haven't you read the blogs? I'm Rory-fucking-Jackson. The only person I've ever loved is myself."

I squinted my eyes at him, noticing the crease between his brow appear again for a split second as he tried to play off the joke. I was quickly becoming aware he didn't have a clue about his small tell, and it made me feel like I had a piece of him no one else did.

This time when I touched his chest I used it to balance on my pumps as I pushed up on my tiptoes to kiss him. I kept myself in check, not slipping my tongue in his mouth like I ached to, but inside teased his lips with mine just enough to make him sigh. Pulling back, I locked onto his blue eyes. "Fuck the blogs. The papers. The magazines. They don't have a clue who you really are."

He smirked. "And you do?"

I licked my lips, happy they tasted like him. "I'm starting to."

His eyes widened as if the prospect was more terrifying than the hits he took on the ice. I laughed, tugging him back toward the party. "It's almost time to clean up. How good are you with your hands?"

"Figured you could answer that by now," he said, following me behind Jeannine's line of tables.

"Jury is still out."

"Ouch. Red, you are hard to please."

"And you're hard—"

"Whoa, kids, we don't need to hear all of that," Jeannine cut me off, and I chuckled. "Or maybe we do." She waggled her eyebrows again as she handed me a dishrag. I smacked her thigh with it before tossing one to Rory.

"You think you can manage to clean some dirty dishes? Or do you have practice?" I asked.

He nodded. "Practice isn't for another few hours. And you know I'm really good at taking care of all things...*dirty*."

Heat rushed to my cheeks as I took up my spot at a full tub of dishes. Those non-existent butterflies were back, and try as I might to explain to them that Rory was nothing but a business arrangement, the fucking things kept on flapping until I felt like I was soaring.

CHAPTER 7

RORY

GAGE CONTROLLED the puck and headed toward the goal, the opposing team's enforcer, Mathison, zeroing in on his back as he took off after him. *Big fucking mistake.* Coach had pulled me off the bench and gave me the green light to play my heart out in this game.

I raced across the ice and crashed into the shithead just as he jerked his stick in front of Gage's skate. The punk went down so hard his helmet smacked off the ice with an audible crack, but Gage barely missed a beat, regained his footing and passed the puck to Warren who shot it in for a goal to tie up the score.

"Fuck yeah!" I screamed, fist bumping Gage's glove and then Warren's as we rounded the ice for the next faceoff. The crowd roared, fueling me with the kind of adrenaline that only hockey could give me.

The Blackhawks—damn them—held their ground, their goalie blocking two more attempts. Sweat soaked everything underneath my gear, pushed harder than I had in weeks. That was the thing about this game; the second Coach said I couldn't play it, only made me want it that much more. I shredded the ice, knocking players into the boards, on their backs, and anywhere an opportunity presented itself. No one was getting at one of my guys, not today.

The breath was cold and quick in my lungs as I flew across the ice, slamming a guy into the boards before he could do the same to Warren. As the ref called offsides, the whistle blowing so we could faceoff at the blueline, a flash of red hair caught my eye. I looked up at the glass and nearly fell on my ass. It was a rare occasion that I'd seen Paige outside of her usual business attire, but seeing her in *my* jersey? Holy fucking shit it was the sexiest thing I'd ever seen. And it wasn't like there weren't fourteen other puck bunnies wearing the same number in the stands because there was. It just looked ten times hotter on *Paige*.

Was that because we'd struck a deal? Because she'd been off limits until recently? Because she was out of my league in too many ways to count? Or was it because ever since I'd gotten that first taste of her in the penthouse, she was all I could think about? Her scent filled my head even though it'd been two days since I'd seen her last. Her laugh echoed in my ears despite the action of the game surrounding me. The woman was under my skin all the ways I'd never thought would happen and I hadn't even fucked her yet.

"Rory!" Gage shouted, snapping me out of thoughts. "Get your fucking head in the game!" He pointed at a defenseman going after one of our wings, and I bolted toward him, barely stopping him before he got our guy on his back.

Fuck. Lock it up, man!

Paige wasn't the first gorgeous woman to show up to watch me play. Hell no. Beautiful women went hand and hand with being a Shark. Not once had I ever let any of them distract me and yet one glimpse of Paige and I was out of position and out of my fucking mind.

I flexed every single one of the muscles I spent hours at the gym sculpting, pushing myself harder than ever, forcing myself to focus on the game and ignore the redhead in the stands. I swore I could hear her screaming my name over anyone else in the crowd, but that was impossible. *Fuck, I was in trouble.*

Smack! Another goon bashed against the boards, dropping to the ice after my bone-crushing hit. I grunted, adjusting my mouthguard that had come loose underneath my helmet. In the two seconds it took to move it in place, I glanced upward where I knew she was in the stands. I just wanted a glimpse of that fiery hair, those emerald eyes...the man chatting her up as he stood over her in the aisle. *Motherfucker was* leaning...*coming on to* my *woman.* A rage I was all too familiar with bubbled near the surface, the urge to leap the boards and let the guy know who the fuck he was talking to, battled in my head.

"Jackson!" Coach yelled this time, and my head snapped around, following his angry face to his jerking hand motioning toward the opposite end of the ice. Before I could skate two inches Gage had been taken down so hard I fucking winced. The player stole the puck while Gage tried to recover, and shot it in for a goal. The buzzer sounded at the same time the lamp lit, the sound shoving my heart to the bottom of my gut as the game ended 3-2.

I skidded to a stop near Gage. "Fuck, man is your shoulder okay?"

Gage ripped his helmet off, skating toward the bench. "Fine." His sharp tone told me to leave him the fuck alone, so I did.

My stomach rolled during the end-of-game niceties. How the fuck had I just let that happen?

"Damn, Rory, what the hell?" Warren asked when we'd made it back to the locker room.

"I—"

"Jackson!" Coach yelled before I could get an answer out. He stomped toward me, and I straightened like he was a four-star general. "What happened out there? You leave your brain in the fucking clouds?"

"No, sir."

"You hungover?"

"No, sir. I haven't had a drop since last week!" I took a deep breath, clenching my hands into fists, so I didn't snap. He had the right to be pissed. I'd gotten distracted and lost us the game.

"You better pray a story doesn't come out about you getting smashed at a bar last night because I will bench you the rest of the season, do you understand? Own up to your shit before you even think about lying to me."

I gave him one nod, holding my ground. It was the truth. I hadn't even been to a bar since the night before the first charity gala I'd attended for Paige.

Paige. The guy. Fuck, that is what had distracted me. Even if for only a few moments, I'd been consumed by jealousy enough to cost us the fucking game. I needed to get a grip on my balls before I lost them.

Coach sighed, the vein throbbing in his forehead turning a less angry shade of purple. "Fine. Next time." He looked at Gage and Warren who stood silently next to me. "We'll get them next time."

"Fuck yeah, we will," Warren said.

"I'll make sure of it," I added.

Coach nodded before stomping back to his office, probably to break something. I hated that my temper was yet again almost costing me the only thing I was ever good at but fuck me it wasn't like I could control it. I was trying and thought the deal with Paige was going to help. Not once did I think she'd have the power to *exacerbate* it.

"What happened?" Gage asked, his tone easier than it had been on the ice.

"I fucked up."

"I get that. Again. But I've never seen you lose it in a game like that before."

"I got...distracted."

"By what?"

I cut my eyes to him before I wiped the sweat from my face with a towel.

"Um, Rory?" Warren pointed behind me toward the hallway entrance. "Towel boy says there is a redhead outside asking for you?"

Gage shifted his weight. "Do not fucking tell me that is Paige out there." He pointed a meaty finger at the door, his massive gun flexing more than necessary.

Shit. "It could be any redhead."

Gage's jaw flexed. "Is it *Bailey's* redhead?"

I patted my bare chest with the towel, chuckling. "Technically she's *my* redhead now."

He raked his fingers through his black hair, spinning so his back was toward me. "What the fuck are you *doing*, man?"

"At least it's not your nanny," Warren snorted, and I hissed. The look Gage flashed him was so not one I'd ever want shot at me. Warren raised his hands and backed away slowly.

"Explain," Gage said, looking at me.

I shrugged. "Paige and I—"

"How is that even the start of a sentence for you?" Gage cut me off. "You don't ever do, *and I's.*"

"I do now." Damn, I sounded defensive even to me.

His eyes trailed me for a second before something clicked and he burst out laughing.

"What?" I snapped after two minutes of straight laughing from him.

"You are so fucked, man."

"How so?"

"You've got it bad. And for that woman? You know who she is right? Like, you *know*—"

"Yeah. I know."

"And you know if you fuck this up it won't just be you who takes the hit in the press. It'll be on her, too."

"Aware."

He sucked in a deep breath. "I hope you know what you're doing, bro. Because I swear if you hurt Bailey's best friend, she'll kill me just for being associated with you."

"Got it. If I fuck up with Paige, there will be an entire mob of people coming after me. Check. Anything else, *Dad?*"

He slit his eyes at me. "Yeah." He stepped closer, lowering his voice. "Do yourself a favor and *don't* fuck it up. Not for everyone else, but for you."

I smirked up at him, opening my arms. "You want to hug this shit out, man?"

He punched me in the chest before flipping me off and walking toward the showers. I was covered in sweat and grime, but I didn't want to keep her waiting outside the locker room door. Pushing it open, I found her leaning casually against the wall next to it. The tight jeans she wore tucked into a pair of flat, black leather boots only made her look that much more fuckable in my jersey. A slew of other puck bunnies hollered for me from across the hallway, but I only had eyes for one woman. *That* had never happened.

"You called?" I asked, my tone sharp from the bullshit of the game and locker room ambush.

She straightened, shoving her hands in her pockets. "I wanted to see if you'd be up for dinner after you were done in there?" She eyed the locker room. "Thought you might want to talk about the game."

A muscle in my jaw clenched as I gritted my teeth.

"Or not," she said. "Never mind. I shouldn't have come." She turned and took several steps away from me. It only took one quick reach to grab her and pull her back.

"Don't. I'm just pissed about the game."

"What happened?" she asked, her voice soft.

I rolled my eyes. "Fucking question of the day and you're the answer."

Her mouth popped into the shape of an O. "What?"

I cocked an eyebrow at her. "Who was that guy talking to you?"

She tilted her head, her eyes shifting from me to the side and back again. "You were watching me?"

"I looked up. You were there. So was he."

"Wow. I honestly didn't think there was a thing that could tear your mind from the game. I wouldn't have come." She shook her head. "Thanks for blaming me though." She spun around again, stomping with more determination toward the exit.

I had to jog to catch up to her. "Stop."

She jerked out from under my touch. "No, *you* stop! Don't you get it?" She touched the center of my chest; her fingers cool against the Under Armour t-shirt I had on over my still heated skin. "This?" she smacked my chest. "Right here? This anger you carry around with you every single place you go? That's the root of every single problem in your life. It's the reason why you need me in the first place."

I kept my jaw locked, the adrenaline from the game, her words, fucking all of it surged with no place to unleash.

"And the guy I was talking to?"

My fist clenched, shaking at my side despite knowing I had no reason to be this jealous. Sure, we had a contract that said she was mine for three months, but it wasn't real. None of it was.

"He's worked at my company for a decade. I spotted him and asked how his daughter was doing." Her eyes dropped to where my fist hung, and she traced her fingertips over it. "Rory you're shaking."

"Game. Adrenaline." I grunted the words out like a fucking caveman.

She didn't buy it for a second, those sharp green eyes not missing one piece of myself that I tried to keep buried underneath the rage. Stepping closer, she moved my fist to the small of her back, slipping her arms around my neck as she reached up on her tiptoes to brush her lips against mine.

I didn't move. I couldn't. A battle raged inside me. One where I knew I was starting to care about this woman way more than I should. Better, *safer* to walk away from it all right now. Tear up the contract and ice my body for a few months to recover from the flames that licked my skin whenever she was close.

"Rory," she sighed name, the tips of her breasts barely grazing my chest as she tried to kiss me again.

"I'm all sweaty."

"I don't care."

"People can see," I managed to say, my muscles unlocking a fraction of an inch as I thought about the crowd of bunnies and reporters just on the other side of the hall.

"Let them."

Those two words, paired with the intensity in her green eyes, broke down whatever gate had held me frozen. I gripped her hips and pressed her against the wall, slanting my mouth over hers. She gasped but opened up for me, tilting her head backward to give me a better angle to stroke her mouth more deeply. Our tongues rubbed and rolled as I fused the only parts of us that our very public location would allow.

Fuck she tasted delicious, and the feel of her body, soft and pliant beneath mine turned the rage in my blood to pure *need*.

"Rory!" I jolted out of our embrace at the sound of Gage's voice.

"Fuck!" I screamed. "Next person who yells my name like that is getting punched in the fucking throat!"

Gage rounded the corner. "Hi Paige," he said in the tone he only reserved for ladies. "Asshole, coach wants you."

I nodded. "Perfect. Like chewing me out in front of the team wasn't enough, now I get to have the private office lecture."

Paige hissed, squeezing my fingers. "Is that worse?"

Gage nodded, and I flipped him off. "I'll see you after?" I asked Paige.

"I'll be here." She smiled up at me, the flush in her cheeks still warm from our kiss.

Gage sighed so loud I'm sure his daughter heard it back home. I walked passed him, ignoring his damn near motherly look of concern as I made my way to the locker room, passing a line of high-maintenance puck bunnies.

"Who is the new bunny?" Linda asked just as I jerked open the door. I clenched my eyes shut and tilted my head toward the ceiling as if asking God *why tonight?*

I had no one to blame but myself. *Dip your dick in crazy twice, shame on you...*

"Not that it's any of your business," I said, letting the door shut, revealing where she leaned in the same spot Paige had been not minutes ago. Coach would be pissed I kept him waiting, but I needed to clear this up before it got out of hand. "She's not a bunny," I continued. "Her name is Paige and she's my..." I swallowed hard. "Girlfriend."

Linda's eyes flew wide as she pressed off the wall. "You don't do girlfriends."

I squinted at the blonde. "You've got no idea what I do."

"Don't I?" She reached out to touch me, and I backed away, my hand on the locker room handle like it was a safety net.

"You really don't." I sighed, not wanting to be a complete dick. "Look, Linda. It was over a year ago. And it was nice, but people change."

"People like you never change, Rory. You're a player. You like variety. I like to provide a flavor on a rotation."

I shook my head. "Not going to happen. Ever. Again. I've tried to explain that to you numerous times. Don't make me have this conversation again." I jerked open the door and let it swing shut behind me.

I sighed as I walked toward coach's office. Who knew being someone's sex-toy for a few months could cause such trouble.

CHAPTER 8

PAIGE

"WHERE DID YOU DISAPPEAR TO?" My father asked, walking with his hands clasped behind his back as we made our weekly walk through the production floors.

He'd been raving about the success of the employee appreciation event, and I hadn't for a second thought he'd noticed my short absence there when I'd followed Rory to his car to collect our freshly signed contract. I swallowed hard.

"What do you mean?" Damn. It didn't matter if I was twenty-eight—when my father got dangerously close to exposing a secret of mine, I was sixteen again, denying his accusations of smelling pot in my bedroom. Jeannine's doing, of course.

"You disappeared for a short time after the winner of your raffle was announced. Was there a problem between some our guests that had to be handled privately?"

I sighed. If the problem was Rory's ability to get me wet with a glance, then yes, absolutely there had been an issue between the guests. "Something like that. Nothing to worry over. I returned as quickly as I was able. The event proceeded without a hitch."

"Did you have to keep it a secret?"

I froze in my tracks outside one of the think-tank rooms which held a handful of our top inventors dreaming up new lines of products for future production.

He noticed my lack of presence at his side after a few moments and backtracked to me. "Honestly, Paige, I thought we were beyond that."

What the hell did he know? I thought about the contract, nestled safely inside my private vault at home. There was no way he'd ever find it. Unless Rory had told someone...

"The secret raffle you held without running it by me first?"

I sighed audibly and straightened myself. "Oh—"

"Good Lord, what did you think I spoke of? You're as white as a sheet."

"Nothing. I didn't know I needed your approval to hold a raffle. If you don't agree with the use of funds, I'd be happy to replace them from my personal account."

He smiled and gently clutched my shoulder. "No, of course, you don't have to run things by me. I would've preferred a heads up though. If only to prep the reporter from the *Seattle Times* who covered the event. He asked for my comment on it, and I had to hustle for words."

"Well, you're used to that." I chuckled in an attempt to shake off the panic still clinging to my insides.

"True, but do try and tell me next time."

"Of course." And in two and a half months he wouldn't have to worry about that sort of thing—well, he would, but it wouldn't be an obligation on my part.

"You changed that woman's life, you know?"

I pressed my lips together, recalling the tears in her eyes when she'd opened the white envelope containing the check I'd made out to her on the company's behalf. The twelve thousand wasn't a blip in the account we held strictly for charitable organizations and morale booster funds for our employees—but it had made an impact on her and her family.

"She won't have to return to the shelter for quite some time." I placed my hand on the knob to the think-tank room.

"That's my Paige. Saving one hungry soul at a time."

"You make it all possible."

"Nonsense. I never handed you your position or the foresight to use it for good in such ways that you do. I wish I could take credit for it. Honestly, I do, but you've carved out this path for yourself. Earned it, every step of the way."

My chest swelled with pride as it always did when I received confirmation for making my father proud—one of my life's ambitions since birth. My aspirations had taken on a new role several years back when I realized the power, I'd have once my father retired—and in that realization, my shelter idea was born. It was so close to fruition. I'd had plans drawn up for the first building and was actively seeking the perfect location.

Now I just had to make sure and not ruin everything.

I pushed open the door, startling a few of the inventors who crowded around a table in the center of the room, touch pad screens and stylus' spread across it. Several computer monitors had graphic designs of what looked to be a new version of the exersaucer—though from the looks of it the item was more complex than the simple entertainment-containment we sold now. My thoughts drifted to Bailey— Lettie would be too big for such a contraption—but the baby on the way? It could be the perfect present. I blinked away the thoughts, smiling as I knew the item wouldn't be in production for at least a year if it ever cleared the board. Still, always good to keep an eye out for my favorite mother to be.

We talked shop for several minutes, listening to the inventor's frustrations with locking mechanisms and educational tools capable of insertion in the materials available. After a good round of reassurance and encouragement from my father and myself, we left them to their work, and with the promise they had our every confidence.

Something my father taught me long before I ever considered taking a business course—employees are the lifeblood of the corporation. Without them, everything falls apart. Ensuring our faith in them and handing out credit where it was due was as much a part of our company's success as the products we sold.

"I'm eager to see that one in production." He said as we walked the halls again.

"Me as well. It'll be a new wave of educational toys combined with the safety of the child using it."

"I wonder when you'll get to purchase one for yourself."

I choked on my own tongue.

Dad laughed and raised his hands in defense. "Sorry. Your mother won't stop moping about no grandchildren on the horizon."

I scoffed. It's not like I didn't *want* children...someday, but I hadn't even thought of settling down. Not that I had a man to do it with currently anyway.

Rory's face flashed behind my eyelids, and I clenched them shut. *Why, heart, why?* It had latched onto him in the last few times I'd seen him, growing deeper each time—not love—but *hope*. Hope for something more.

Just because he can make you wet in under a minute doesn't make him your happily ever after.

But it wasn't just his incredible sex appeal that spurred the stupid hope—it was the way he'd seemed genuinely interested in learning what I cared about, like showing up at the event and going so far to donate. He was still the bad boy the media painted him to be, but he'd taken an effort in my world to get to know me, and that counted for something.

Plus, there was the episode at the hockey game. I'd never seen him more flustered in my life, and I'd been watching him play for years. And he credited *me* for the distraction. That meant something—I just didn't know if it was good or bad.

"What about Rory Jackson?" Father interrupted my internal battle.

"What about him?"

"Does he have affections for you?"

"What would make you say that?"

"His contribution to the event alone would be enough, but his speech...he specifically singled you out in an effort to please you." He arched a knowing brow at me, which told me he already knew the truth. Damn. I must've missed a picture online of us kissing—no doubt outside the Shark's locker room. The moment had been so charged, and he'd clearly needed it so badly, I hadn't thought twice. Guess our fake relationship was now up for public scrutiny, including my father's.

"Well, we're...dating." The word tasted dry in my mouth. Dating was such a long shot from what we shared. Lovers would be a closer match—but only because *lusters* wouldn't sound nearly as proper if I said it out loud.

"He didn't shy away from one fan who approached him." He ignored my verbal attachment to the man completely.

I nodded.

"It shocked me. Honestly, when he showed up I was glad for the PR but was terrified he'd cause a scene. The kind of world he lives in...the attention he garners with his short fuse—"

"Father." I huffed. I knew his stance on me dating anyone who drew any kind of unwanted attention. I'd known the rules since I was twelve. Maybe that is why I enjoyed breaking them so much.

"I apologize. It's a habit. I know you're a grown woman, Paige. One I couldn't be more proud of, but you'll always be my baby girl. And I want your future to soar, not get raked through the muck by tabloid reporters who are begging for you to make a mistake."

"Like they do you? That won't change when I become C.E.O. They'll watch my every move just as they have yours our whole lives. Who I date shouldn't matter." *Was I really defending a contracted relationship that was only to benefit each party in different ways? Why did I care so much if my father approved of Rory or not?*

Because he's a good man and no one gave him near enough credit. The truth rang clear in my mind, and damn it, my heart.

"You're right," he continued. "But pairing yourself with someone who has the same heat on them—*more so* because of his celebrity-athlete status and a reputation for trouble finding him wherever he goes—you'll only increase your odds of slipping."

"You have so little faith in me?"

"I have the utmost confidence in you, darling. It's the greasy paparazzi who take an innocent image and tarnish it into something wretched, and even if the story isn't true, it only takes the hint of immorality to bring everything we've worked for crashing down."

"You don't have to keep lecturing me. I'm not a teenager." I'd heard the speech too many times, and the thoughts plagued me on a daily basis—I didn't need it thrown in my face, too.

"You're old enough and smart enough to do what you want. I only want you to be crystal clear on the stakes at risk if you decide to bring that kind of heat on yourself."

My head spun in all different directions, my father's words giving me whiplash. As a dad, he supported my right to choose to do what I pleased. As a C.E.O. he warned me off anything that would come close to putting the company at risk.

I knew damn well my father could say I had a choice all he wanted, but it was the choice *he'd* make that he'd approve of.

"It's not just your image or even the company's at risk," he continued when I hadn't responded. I slit my eyes, catching the tone he often used in the boardroom right before he slammed an ultimatum on the table that no one would dare argue with or try to negotiate out of. He stepped closer to me, placing a hand on my shoulder. "I want you to think very carefully about this before you get in too deep with him."

"Father," I said, matching his tone in a *don't push me* threat.

"Like I said you're your own woman. And who you choose to *date* is up to you, but know this," he dropped his hand. "If that young man has one slip while you are in his presence—one more brawl off the ice, one more incident where he is carted off to jail—I'll cut funding to your pet project. There are consequences when you make foolish choices, Paige."

I gasped, stepping away from him as if he'd stung me. Anger boiled my blood, but I kept my spine straight and my breath even. "The company and its funding will be mine in three months."

Father sighed, tilting his head. "As long as I still think you're capable of running it seamlessly. You take up with this celebrity party-boy and let him sully your reputation this close to the transition? I won't retire. And there will be no more bank for the shelter you're building."

The sting deepened in the center of my chest. I'd seen him use an incredibly stern hand in too many mergers to count, but I'd never expected him to be so strict with me. Not now. Not after everything I'd worked for and proven to him. He'd just taken my arrangement with Rory and upped the ante surrounding it. I never thought the project of my heart would be at risk. For a few fleeting seconds the prospect of ending it before it'd really even began filtered through my mind.

Then, after a few deep breaths, I realized I believed in Rory far too much for that. Plus, there was no denying our connection—contract or not. I wouldn't give up on him so easily, no matter what my father threatened. I wouldn't be the business woman I was today if I fled at the drop of a few harsh words from an older man.

"We should continue if we want to make the rounds on all ten production floors today." I decided to ignore his threat altogether and pressed on to the next think-tank room, effectively ending the conversation. Knots twisted in my shoulders and the tension created an ache at the base of my neck. Father didn't have a clue what had happened between Rory and I—not truly—and I shuddered, thinking of what he'd say if he knew the exact circumstances surrounding our attachment.

Or how close I was to saying *screw the rules* and the risks and the constant looking over my shoulder, and simply dive the fuck in.

We ended the day on the tasting floor, sampling several new batches of our all organic baby food line. It amazed me, the talent we held within the walls of our building, and their abilities to constantly surprise and impress me. The successful approach of combining the freshest, most vibrant ingredients and convenient packaging—all while making sure the food wasn't the slightest bit bland—lifted my spirits considerably.

The conversation with my father still weighed on my mind. I had teams of unbelievable people counting on me, and that wasn't something to stress over. It wasn't a burden. It was a *privilege*, an *honor*. And I knew I'd do my best to accommodate all the wishes of my heart as best as I possibly could—taking care of my employees, giving life to my shelter development, and, hopefully, my commitments to Rory as well.

———

Friday came at the end of a particularly long week—one because of my father's need to prep and grill me on connections and obligations of the company which I'd known for years, and two, because I'd been completely unsuccessful at drowning out my cravings.

Rory Jackson cravings.

And I hated to admit it, but it wasn't all entirely sexual fantasy either. I found myself wondering what he really liked to do for fun—if it went beyond the booze, brawls, and hockey the media constantly reported on.

I walked into *Nine's* a little after five o'clock, the place hopping with activity as opposed to the other night when I'd come much later in the evening. I'd contemplated going home and cracking open the laptop to continue the work week, but I'd quickly dismissed the idea. I'd worked overtime this week, and I needed a drink in the biggest way.

There was shockingly a two-top table available, and I sighed as I sank into the plush chair Jeannine had picked out herself before opening the restaurant. She'd gone over the details with a microscope, controlling every choice in her business from the fisherman who supplied her to the type and weight of the silverware. *Nine's* had a modern style that wasn't pretentious like some fine-dining options tended to be in the city, and it offered a cozy environment where one could eat and drink without cause to put on airs. It was perfectly and absolutely Jeannine's, and I had asked for many pieces of advice when devising my own business plans for the shelter.

"Hi, Paige." A waitress named Olivia who waited on me often set down a scotch and soda in front of me. "Are you dining tonight?"

"Yes. Please tell Jeannine to surprise me." I smiled as I brought the drink to my lips.

"Will anyone else be joining you?" Olivia eyed the empty chair across from me.

I shook my head, and she dashed off to the kitchen. I swirled the liquor in my glass, inhaling the sharp scent, and relished the tension it soothed as the scotch slid down my throat. I kept my cell secured in my bag and hung it on the handle of the chair, resisting the urge to hop on the media-sites and hunt for Rory sightings. I had seen several pictures of us together—outside the Shark's locker room and outside my company's event as well, along with the rumored stories of our relationship, too. We hadn't even had sex yet, and I was turning into a borderline puck bunny, searching for news about him in between actually seeing the man. I contemplated attending the Shark's game next week but quickly quashed the idea. I didn't fully understand what it was about me, or if it had just been that particular day, but I wasn't going to distract him ever again.

I jolted in my seat when another x-rated fantasy clouded my mind, reminding me of the one thing I needed to take just in case I ever did get to make the fantasy a reality. I reached into my purse and grabbed my birth control, cursing myself for getting so caught up in work today I'd forgotten to take it with lunch like I normally did. Oh well, I suppose there was one good thing about Rory's painfully slow pace with me.

One drink later Olivia set down two wedge salads.

"I know Jeannine thinks I don't eat enough greens but this is a little much, don't you think?"

"It's for your guest."

"Oh, I apologize, you must've misunderstood me. No one is joining—"

"Whew. Just in time. Glad you didn't start without me." Rory's voice cut me off as he approached my table, slinging his black leather jacket off and handing it to Olivia's outstretched hands. Had to give the girl credit, she didn't giggle or stammer, simply nodded and took it to the check room. I suppose she was much more accustomed to waiting on celebrities than I was.

Rory sat across from me, instantly picking up his fork and knife, slicing himself a bite of the wedge salad Olivia had set there for him. As if it was normal. As if we'd planned a date. My heart rate doubled like I was back in high school with my first crush.

He took a quick sip of my scotch, grinning at me over the rim. "How was your day, dear?"

Butterflies flapped in my stomach at the sight of his damn smile and those blue eyes locked onto mine. I laughed despite trying not to. "I'm not sure romantic pet names will ever sound normal coming out of your mouth."

He shrugged, taking another bite. "You've got me there...*Red*."

I licked my lips and took another drink, suddenly needing the liquid courage. *He signed a contract to be yours in all kinds of delicious ways for three months! You're beyond dating nerves!*

"You really want to know about my day?" I asked, tinkling the ice in my glass.

"Absolutely. Then I can vent about mine. Isn't that how a relationship works?" He cocked an eyebrow at me, sliding the fork over his lips so slowly I shifted in my seat.

"From what I can remember," I said. It had been years, but honestly, I hadn't had a real relationship in my life. Every single man had treated me with the wholesome, moralistic, political gloves that surrounded my family. They wanted to be president someday, not fuck me until my eyes rolled back in my head. It wasn't even that they put me on a pedestal as much as it was that I was a step on their ladder of success. Rory was different—he might need me to help his image, but his success was his own, and that was something I fiercely admired.

"You're blushing. Again. Something about your workday get you there?" He teased, and I cleared my throat.

"No. It was rather stressful actually." I went on to tell him more than just about today's problems, but the days prior as well. Including when my father had dropped the hammer about what he'd do if Rory and I screwed this up. That little tidbit had Rory's signature crease cinching between his brow for far longer than I'd ever seen before. "In relationships, usually the other person says something," I said after I'd finished venting. "You know, something like *hang in there* or *you did everything right*."

A soft smile wiped the crease away just as Olivia cleared our entrée plates. "I've never been in one so excuse me while I catch up on this crash course."

"Never?" I asked, genuinely shocked. "Not even before you became a coveted Shark?"

He pressed his lips together, finishing his ice water. "Nope."

"I can't tell if that is totally fitting for you, or kind of sad." I chuckled. "Who am I kidding? You're Rory Jackson. Of course it's fitting." I shook my head, my hair brushing my shoulders. Just because I was feeling a deeper connection to the man than what our contract entailed didn't mean the renowned player was reciprocating.

"And what if it wasn't fitting?" He asked, his tone soft and yet gruff. "What if I simply hadn't met someone who I could see a future with?"

I nodded, setting my drink down. "That would make sense."

He parted his lips, something on the tip of that magical tongue of his but Oliva popped up tableside to ask if we wanted dessert, and he clamped his mouth shut. I denied despite knowing Jeannine would send something regardless.

"Rory?" I asked after his crystal blue eyes had stared at the contents of his glass for far too long. He blinked a few times, a deep breath forcing his perfect chest to move down.

"You should shred the contract."

"What?" I choked the word out as if he'd stolen the breath from my lungs. I regained my composure and locked eyes with him. "Are you having second thoughts?" My chest clenched at the mere thought. *Shit. We hadn't had sex yet, and already I was mourning his potential loss.* I was in too deep, and we hadn't truly begun.

"Hell no," he snapped, drowning out my panicked thoughts. "But..."

"I hate that word." Nothing good ever followed it. Not in business, not in life.

"You've got so much to lose, Paige." The use of my proper name versus his preferred *Red* had my stomach sinking. He raked his fingers through his blond hair. "You really want to risk it on a fuck up like me?"

I pursed my lips, clucking my tongue at him like he had me before. "Rory, insecurity doesn't suit you."

"I'm serious. I've got..." he leaned his head closer to me and lowered his voice. "An anger problem."

I gasped, feigning shock.

"Look, I know it's not a shock, but you have to know it's gotten me into trouble more times than I can count. I'd fucking hate myself if I slipped and you lost your dream."

I reached across the table, laying my hand over his. "I don't know where this anger stems from..." I eyed him, giving him an opening to explain if he wanted to. He didn't so I continued. "And I'm a good listener if you ever want to let me in on that little secret, but you have to stop selling yourself so damn short, Rory."

His eyes widened, glancing from our joined hands and back to me as if he didn't know how to respond.

"You have to know I'm an investor," I said, smirking. "I don't get involved in deals I know will go south. You are a good deal, Rory. Hell, you may be the best contract I've ever struck." A flush danced across my cheeks. "Well, I suppose the determining factor is yet to be...*experienced.*"

He licked his lips, stroking the back of my hand with his thumb. "You're incredible. You know that, Red?"

I chuckled. "Now you're just trying to get on my good side."

"I'd like to be on whatever side you'll allow me *in* on." He licked a stray drop of water off the corner of his lip, and I shifted in my seat.

"Truly?" I asked, wondering if I'd read too much into his words. A single nod had my heart flying with anticipation.

"Can I get you two anything else?" Olivia asked as she approached our table.

"Check." We both said in unison.

CHAPTER 9

RORY

DAMN IT. That annoying tightening in my gut was back as I unlocked the door to my loft and motioned Paige inside. Instinct begged me to strip her of her blazer and dress slacks and fuck her against the island in my kitchen. My mouth watered just thinking about it, but my muscles weren't working properly. Where I should be jerking her to me the second she set foot inside my place, I was frozen in the entryway, silently hoping she liked it—hoping she liked *me*.

What the hell, man? You brought her here for one thing! She has practically begged you for it for weeks. If all I had was three months with this girl—hell, less than that now— then I needed to make the best of every single minute.

"This is gorgeous," she said, popping the bubble of silence that had threatened to steal what little manhood I still possessed. *What the fuck was wrong with me?*

I glanced down at my dick, giving him a silent pep talk I'd never needed to before. I'd never waited this long to sleep with a woman, or gotten as close as I had to Paige. Maybe that was the problem. I was used to a quick roll in the sheets before I disappeared into the night, leaving the girls with nothing but a smile and a hotter than hell memory. Each of them knew what they were getting into with me—hell, every blog and gossip site had done the dirty work for me, constantly painting me as the Bruce Wayne of the Sharks.

Paige was different. This wouldn't be one and done. Not even close. And it scared the shit out of me.

"The view is stunning," she said, slowly slipping out of her blazer and dropping it over the arm of my leather sofa as she passed it. She flipped her hair over her shoulder as she reached the floor to ceiling glass doors that lead out to the balcony of my high-rise, grinning at me. "Being a Shark pays off."

I chuckled, shoving my hands in my pockets as I only met her halfway, keeping my distance from her as if touching her would burn me. "I overpaid for this place because of that view." I nodded toward the sparkling lights that lit up the city on the horizon, the night sky black as ink behind it.

She turned toward me. "It must be an instant hit with the bunnies. Bring them up here, take them out there and boom, panties dropped, huh?"

I shook my head. The woman never ceased to surprise me. I never knew what would come out of her mouth and it kept me on my toes more than any chick ever had. "Wouldn't know."

"Ah," she said, pressing her lips together as her eyes trailed my body. "I suppose you wouldn't need a view like this to get a woman into bed."

The nerves in my gut twisted. I needed a fucking drink, but I hadn't had more than one since Coach had ridden me about the game last week. "I've never brought another woman up here."

Paige's red hair trembled as she laughed like I'd cracked a joke. "Yeah, okay."

I shrugged. "Unless you count Lettie."

She glanced around the apartment. "The only woman who has seen your place is Gage's four-year-old?"

I took a step closer to her, licking my lips. "And now, *you*."

The laughter left her eyes, and she sucked in a shaken breath. I didn't need to explain how bringing her here meant more than the terms of our contract, she could see it in my eyes. The woman missed nothing, and honestly, I was getting tired of trying to keep her out.

I finally reached out to her, touching the soft skin of her cheek. "Tell me what you want," I said, wrapping my other hand around the back of her neck, planting slow kisses against the line of her jaw. She arched against me, her breasts lightly grazing my chest and the move shot heat straight to my dick.

"You," she said, her voice breathless as I lightly trailed my tongue down her neck.

I locked eyes with her, finally shaking off the newness of seducing a woman in my place—a woman that mattered to me, whether I wanted to admit it or not—and smirked. "Not enough. I need more."

Her skin tightened under my touch as I roamed my hands over her bare arms, her covered breasts, and her hips. She parted her lips, reaching for mine instead of answering.

I pulled back but pressed my hard dick against her center, the heat scorching even with clothes on. I couldn't fucking wait to rip them off, but I held my ground. She tilted her head backward, sighing from the connection as she dug her fingers into my back.

"Rory," she groaned.

"Tell me," I demanded. She needed to say it. There would be no misunderstandings between us in this department. Period.

"Rory, fuck me." The fierce need in her voice nearly had me coming in my pants it was so fucking hot.

"More," I said, nipping at the skin of her neck.

She sighed, the breath full of frustration as she wiggled against me.

I smirked, loving that she wanted this as badly as me. Contract or not.

"Paige," I said, a warning to my tone as I moved an inch away from her.

She grabbed my hips and jerked me back to her, never losing my eyes. "Rory. I want you to fuck me so well I won't ever forget."

I hissed, the fire in those green eyes blazing in my blood. I threaded my fingers through her hair, arching her head backward. "Is that on your list?"

"You know it is."

Slanting my mouth over hers, I pulled her close, relishing every single soft curve she had. Slowly I pulled her silk shirt over her head, tossing it to the floor before I unbuttoned her pants, easily slipping the wide legs over her black heels which she left on.

"Fucking perfect." I stayed on my knees, taking in every inch of her smooth skin covered only by the black lace of her bra and panties. Grabbing a handful of her gorgeous ass, I pulled her close and pushed her panties to the side just enough to kiss her already wet pussy.

"Oh, God," she moaned, fisting my hair as I dipped my tongue inside her.

"You taste fucking divine." Sweet—even better than the last time—and hot and *mine*. I hooked one hand underneath her knee and rested it over my shoulder, loving the bite of pain from her high heel on my back. I supported her balance with nothing but my arms and the grip on her hips, and the angle it gave me was worth every fucking day I spent at the gym.

"Rory." My name was a whisper on her lips, and with the taste of her on my tongue, I was ready to sink deep inside her until *Rory* was the only word she knew.

I hummed against her wetness, growling as I pulled away and slipped a finger inside her. She ground against it with a greedy hunger that only made me harder. Any more and I would bust through my pants. "You're there already," I said, sucking in a sharp breath when she clenched around my fingers as I added another. Her response was so open, so honest, so incredibly hot that it would have taken me to my knees if I wasn't already there.

She only responded with a moan as I pushed deeper inside her. "How badly do you want this?"

"God, Rory. *Please.*"

Fuck, Paige. The ache in her voice, the wet tightness of her body, she was so much better than every fantasy of mine she'd starred in. When she begged me like that, fuck it only made me want to make her come every day for the rest of her life.

Wait, what?

She rolled against my hand, another moan ripping from her lips, successfully grounding me in the present. I pressed deeper and sucked her clit into my mouth, flicking it with my tongue with just enough pressure until I felt her legs tremble around me. I tightened my hold on her as she flew apart around my mouth because while I'd pushed her over the edge, I would never let her fall.

"Rory!" She screamed and damn near ripped my hair

out as she continued to come, aftershocks rippling around me. I gently stroked her before lightly kissing her soft, hot skin until she had come down. Unhooking her leg from over my shoulder, I didn't let her stand on her own for long. I swept an arm beneath her knees and gently sat her on the couch.

Her eyes were hooded, and lust filled as I slowly peeled off my clothes. She took in every inch of my body, and I resisted the urge to flex. I was proud of my body, of the lengths I went to striving for my best, but the look in her eyes made me feel like a God. "We're just getting started, Red."

She licked her lips as I dropped my black briefs and scooped her off the couch. I could've easily fucked her there, or hell, I could've taken a left and went to the bedroom. But this was *Paige,* and no ordinary place would do.

I opened the balcony door and carried her out into the crisp Seattle air.

"Rory, what if someone sees?" The excitement in her eyes didn't match the concern in her tone.

I gently set her on her feet, sliding her panties down her legs and over her heels. "Do you trust me?" I asked, kissing my way back up her leg until I'd reached her mouth. I threaded my fingers through her hair, holding my breath as I waited for her answer—somehow, it seemed more important than anything else I'd ever needed before.

She worried her bottom lip between her teeth for only a moment before she wrapped her arms around my neck and hopped, locking her ankles around my back. "Yes," she said before pressing her lips against mine.

I held her underneath her perfect ass, slowly guiding us until her back pressed against the glass. She hissed from the cold on her hot skin, but the way she arched against my hard cock said she liked it.

"Say it again," I demanded, breaking our kiss as I shifted her above me, the tip of my dick brushing her wet center.

She shuddered around me, her eyes taking more time to focus as if we were high. Fuck, maybe we were. Maybe she was a dream.

"I trust you."

I hissed, her words hitting the center of my chest. I slid inside her and growled as her tight walls hugged every inch of my dick with slick, molten heat. She clawed at my back as she rocked her hips up and down, matching each thrust I gave her with vigor. This woman was a match for me in every way, giving more than she took, meeting every challenge with one of her own.

"Fuck, Red. You feel amazing." The words came out more like a growl, but I couldn't help it. Something primal inside of me wanted to claim this woman for my own in a way I'd never felt before. With each of her moans, I felt like fucking Superman, the gratification of her clenching around me, over and over again, was better than winning ten championships. Better than the feel of a good fight, better than the ice beneath my skates and a stick in my gloved hands. My blood was on fire, my skin electric, all because of *her*.

I pulled my head back, just enough to catch her eyes. They locked onto mine as I slowed our pace and I knew she could see through me, see where my head was at. The moment was charged, a current connecting us on more levels than physical.

Fuck, I'm a goner.

I shifted, holding her weight with only one arm, taking my free hand to cup her cheek as I slowly pumped inside her, never losing those gorgeous green eyes of hers. Her breath quickened, another wave crashing over my dick as she tightened around me. The look in her eyes before she gently set her mouth against mine had me crashing right alongside her—coming in the instant she did—and it was so hard I nearly lost all balance I had.

Shit! I flinched as the blood rushed back to my brain and I realized how fucking perfect I felt—*bare*—inside her.

"What is it?" she asked breathlessly.

"I didn't grab a condom," I said, glancing down like I could magically turn back the moment. Panic rippled through my blood as all the heat from my body drained. I cursed myself for getting so lost in the moment with her, something that had never happened before. I always remembered to wrap it up.

She chuckled, the motion making me hard again, and a mental battle instantly warred as I slowly moved inside her because it felt so fucking good. "I'm on birth control, and I'm clean," she said and the heat came rushing back in such a huge relief I almost high fived her.

"Me too. The clean part at least."

"Well, now that we've got that settled."

I grinned, steadying myself, and held her close. With the city I loved at my back, and still being inside the woman of my dreams, I realized just how absolutely fucked I was.

There would never be another woman who saw the heart of me, past the uniform and the trophies. Paige didn't need my money, my name, my position—hell, she wanted me in spite of those things. She rocked me to my core, more than physically—though I wasn't sure I'd ever be able to have sex again without seeing her face, calling out her name. She knew my demons and held me anyway. She trusted me, believed in me. I hadn't just crossed off an item on her list—

I'd let her *in*. All the way in. And now I didn't want to let her go. Ever.

And I had less than three months to get her to feel the same way.

I kissed her again before leaning my forehead against hers, allowing my eyes to close as we caught our breath.

CHAPTER 10

PAIGE

DON'T THINK ABOUT RORY. Don't think about Rory.

I chanted the mantra over and over to myself, trying to drown out the still hot and fresh memories from my mind. Rory's Greek-God-like body, cut in all the right ways, moving in all the right ways against me, inside me...on the balcony, in his bed, in his kitchen. I was still sore, and it had been two days. The best sex of my life by far, but I couldn't deny something more had happened than just world-bending orgasms that night. Something had shifted inside me, and it wasn't just his perfect cock. The last piece of me that had been holding back, keeping Rory locked in a file with nothing but a contract, fell. *I* fell. And it had left me terrified.

Sweat popped on the back on my neck as my skin flushed from the memory and again I forced myself to concentrate. If I didn't, I'd end up blurting out how perfect Rory's body was at the press conference.

Focus!

I gripped my iPhone; the prepared speech pulled up on the screen as I stepped out of the company car. This—right here, this was where I would make a difference. Where I would leave my mark. Tears bit the backs of my eyes as I took in the perfect location for my shelter, but I kept them on lockdown right alongside thoughts of Rory.

A warm shiver danced across my skin just *thinking* his name.

My black pumps crunched against the gravel as I made my way to the massive brick building that had once been a company that made phonebooks. The place had long been on the market, and it needed work, but I could see the potential where other buyers hadn't. I'd signed the papers last week.

A slew of reporters waited outside the front of the building ready to take my statements on what exactly I was doing with the place. The site was also crowded with workers, already implementing the plans I'd discussed with the contractor, electrician, and code manager I'd hired. The hustle of steps and sounds of power tools thrilled me to the point of being giddy. My dream finally bursting with life. It wouldn't be long before it would serve this community in ways no shelter ever had before.

"Ms. Turner!" Reporters started shouting the minute I stepped up the concrete stairs to address them.

"Yes?" I pointed to the first journalist I'd heard.

The crowd hushed and waited. "Are the rumors about you and Mr. Jackson true?"

My mouth went dry, but I straightened my spine, offering them a soft smile. "This is a press conference to discuss the objectives of the newest undertaking at Cran-Baby Organics, not a tell all on my personal life." Not that I was trying to hide Rory—we'd been caught on camera holding hands and even kissing—but I wasn't prepared to be vetted about him here. This was about my shelter, not my "relationship."

The fact that I still couldn't think of it as a real relationship had my stomach sinking in ways it had no right to. Rory and I had made a deal. A business deal, and just because something had changed inside me that night, didn't mean Rory's feelings had. He was still the notorious bad boy of the Shark's and would return to his playboy status once our three months were up. I'd simply have to guard my heart more carefully and enjoy the time I had.

Keep telling yourself that.

And here I was thinking about Rory when I should be announcing my dream project. I shifted on my pumps, maintaining my smile.

"Apologies, Ms. Turner," the reporter said. "Can't help the curiosity."

I nodded. Rory needed the good press, too, and who was I to not answer one little question that could help his image in the media? "Quite all right," I said, smoothing down my fitted gray T which laid over my nicest blue jeans. I may be in heels, but I came here to get my hands dirty. "Mr. Jackson and I *are* together. Now they aren't rumors, and we can discuss the matter at hand." I motioned to the gorgeous building behind me.

The reporter grinned, and I took the silence to explain the intricacies of the project. By the time I was done, I had nearly cried twice. God, my emotions were all over the place. "As you can tell," I dabbed at the corner of one eye that had traitorously given up one tear. "You can see how important this is to me, and to CranBaby Organics. This will be no ordinary shelter. It won't simply feed and house Seattle's homeless. It will give them resources, outreach programs, and training to get back the lives they once had. Our city deserves it, but more so, *they do*."

A round of applause drowned out the sounds of the workers and volunteers inside the building, and I flashed the reporters my media worthy smile—not too much teeth, just enough lip. And after a quick round of questions, I thanked them all for coming and turned to step inside the building.

It was one thing to have a dream, and quite another to see it come to life.

The main level was perfect—a wide open floorplan that would be constructed into a warm, welcoming, not at all clinical lobby for those in need. I'd told my contractor I wanted them to feel as if they were checking into a hotel, not a poorly funded charity.

People hustled back and forth, carrying two by fours and tools and charts and wires. The buzz was intoxicating enough to steal my breath. Or maybe it was the face I easily recognized carting two massive pieces of wood over his shoulders that stopped my heart.

"Rory?" My voice squeaked from the shock of seeing him here.

He followed my voice until he spotted me standing there gaping at him. "Just a sec!" He called, hurrying across the massive room to drop the boards in a fastly growing pile. He strolled back toward me, his jeans dirtied with sawdust and grime. The white T-shirt he wore clung to his rock hard abs from the sweat dripping slowly down his arms.

The closer he got to me the harder it was to breathe, as if my heart filled up my entire chest so there was no room for air. Kissing my cheek once he reached me, I stood frozen.

He glanced down at my pumps before returning those

crystal blue eyes to mine. "You know how fond I am of those," he pointed to them. "But they aren't really what I'd have you working in here."

I arched an eyebrow at him. "Oh, so you're the boss now?"

He smirked. "You like it when I'm in control." He shifted closer to me. He smelled like fresh cut wood and one hundred percent man. "Admit it."

I bit my bottom lip, the pain sharpening the wits I always lost around him. "What are you doing here?" I smiled as I gestured to the building around us.

"No practice today."

"So on all non-practice days, you roam the city looking for charities in need?" I teased.

"Only ones who are headed up by gorgeous redheads." A flush danced across my cheeks, and he grinned. "This is important to you. That makes it important to me."

I swallowed hard, squinting at him as if that would make the truth easier to see. Was he saying that because it's what a man in a relationship would say? Was he only behaving this way because it had been in our contract that we must act like a real couple? The lines were now so blurry I didn't know how to draw new ones, and I wasn't sure I wanted to.

Suddenly, the last thing I wanted to do was work. The only thing I wanted making me sweat was Rory.

"Later," he whispered as if he could read my mind.

"Excuse me?" I asked, breathless.

He flashed me a knowing look and lightly trailed his fingers over the skin of my collarbone. "Later," he repeated. "Now, we have work to do." He winked and turned around, walking back across the room to where he'd dropped off the boards.

For a few moments, I stood rooted to the spot as I watched him ask my head contractor what needed to be done. The air grew thin again, and my heart took off like it had just joined a race. The feeling—the consuming, electric, pulsing, aching, *need*—filled every inch of available space inside my soul and it only awoke in the presence of one man. Rory.

Oh holy hell. I'm in love with him.

Somehow the crush I'd had for years had grown into something deeper, more meaningful as my eyes were opened to not just the guy I saw at Bailey and Gage's, but the man he really was. The truth of the thought only added to the butterflies in my stomach followed quickly by a generous splash of ice cold fear. I was in love with a man I'd contracted to be with me for three months, and three months only.

A bad boy shark and a proper corporation princess had no real business being together. Nothing real enough to last. Did we?

"You coming, Red?" Rory's voice drew me out of myself, and I tossed him a fake smile. The crease between his brow flashed. "You all right?"

"Yes, of course. Let's get to work." I hurried past him, seeking out my electrician and silently thanking him for using big words I could barely understand. It was enough to silence the excitement and fear blaring in my head, screaming the only thing that mattered at the moment.

I was in love, and it had an expiration date.

After working half the day away, I hadn't successfully buried my worries, but I had successfully gotten good and dirty. Sweat soaked my jeans and shirt, the back of my neck, and my hands were covered in grime, but it felt good. The grit was a testament to how much we accomplished today and watching the crew rally and put into motion plans I'd dreamt of for years was a pile of icing on one hell of a cake.

"Let me take you home," Rory said as we walked out of the building. The sun hung low in the sky fighting the good fight before night claimed it.

My heart fluttered in my chest, the same damn way it had every time he'd spoken to me since I realized I'd fallen for him. "All right," I said and waved off my driver.

The ride to my place was silent save for the few times Rory complimented me on my eye for details. It was like I didn't have a clue how to act around him now that my heart had latched on to the one man I'd basically hired to use for sex.

For God's sake, he's not a prostitute. It was a mutually agreed upon contracted relationship, not a porn. Well, it did have some of the better aspects of porn, but still. I should have known this was going to happen. I'd had a crush on the man for *years*, and now he was here, with me, and so much better than anything I could have ever imagined.

I clenched my eyes shut, breathing a sigh of relief when Rory's driver pulled us up to my house. "Thank you again for showing up today, Rory. It was above and beyond." *And totally pushed me over the damn ledge I'd teetered on with my feelings for you.*

"You don't want me to come in?" He asked, climbing out of the car behind me.

I floundered around in my own head before I found my voice. "Of course I do. It's just...I'm all dirty and—"

He cut my words off with a kiss, his tongue slipping inside my mouth like he'd always belonged there. I immediately melted into his embrace, forgetting about all the reasons I shouldn't—like how much of a hot sweat-soaked mess I was or how he was stealing my heart instead of striking off items on a list.

"Let's get wet," he said, smacking my butt as he walked passed me toward my front door.

I gaped after him, my heart racing in my chest from his kiss. I unlocked the door and led him to the master bath in my bedroom. He closed the door behind me, locking it as if someone could waltz in at any moment. Or perhaps he was worried I'd run and wanted to keep me there. Both weren't going to happen. Rory didn't need bolts to keep me, hell, all he had to do was ask, and I'd truly be his in a heartbeat. But what was I thinking? The man was performing his contractual obligations well, and that's all.

"I can't believe you wore those heels," he said, eyeing my pumps again. "I want to make a rule here and now. You're *never* allowed to wear those to a game, okay? They *kill* me." He hissed, slipping his hands underneath the hem of my T and pulling it over my head.

"Am I *allowed* to come back to a game?" I asked, the notion shocking me with excitement. I hadn't wanted to distract him ever again, but damn did I love to watch him play.

He scrunched his eyebrows at me. "I want you in the stands."

"You do?" The hopefulness in my tone was so obvious I was shocked he didn't pick up on it.

"Hell yes. I won't fuck up again. Well, I won't as long as you don't wear these." He tugged each pump off before sliding me out of my jeans. I took my time peeling his clothes off, relishing the way his rock hard muscles felt underneath my fingertips.

"Deal," I finally said when I'd stripped him bare. I reached inside my shower and turned it to hot, popping the clasp of my bra after I was finished. A quick drop of my panties—which earned me a growl from Rory—and I stepped in.

The warm drops of water hit my skin and soothed the tense muscles underneath. When Rory's hands gently gripped my hips, my body coiled for an entirely new reason. I turned around to face him, suddenly beyond grateful I'd bought a house with a massive stand up marble shower. I had often thought it was a tad too big for only me but with Rory's large frame in front of me, I knew it was worth it. He seemed to do that with every facet of my life—find the big, empty spaces and consume them until everything felt just right.

He smiled down at me, lightly teasing my skin as the water rolled over us both. Reaching over me, he grabbed the bottle of lavender body wash I had on the shelf and squirted a mountain in his hand. Rubbing his hands together, he quickly created a lather which he immediately smoothed over my skin.

"So," he said, working his hands up and down my body like he'd memorized it. "Is this on your list?"

I sucked in a deep breath, gathering some of the suds and swiping them across his chest. Damn the man was cut like he was carved out of the same marble as the shower. "No," I said, sliding my hands across his lickable V lines. "But I'm starting to think it should've been number one."

He chuckled, the sound igniting my insides as much as his touch. A moan escaped my lips when he threaded his fingers through my hair, his body close enough I could feel the hardness of his cock against me.

"Can I see it yet?" He asked, his tone slightly gravelly.

I bit my lip and shook my head.

"Come on," he begged. "Give me *something*."

A deeper blush than I thought possible flushed my entire body.

Rory tilted my chin up, forcing me to meet his eyes. "How are you embarrassed? You think there is something you could throw at me that I couldn't handle?"

I pressed my lips together to hold back a laugh. "Not a chance." I had every confidence Rory could check off all the items left on my list within a matter of days if I asked him to.

"Hey," he said when I'd dropped my eyes once again. "What is it?" He wrapped a soapy arm around my hip, pulling me against him.

I wanted to tell him the truth. Wanted to say I couldn't stop falling for him, that I'd already fallen too hard, and I was scared to death of what would happen to my heart when our arrangement was up.

"Paige," he said before I could find the courage to say a word. "I'm here. With you. And there isn't a thing on that list of yours that you should be embarrassed over. In fact, I think you'd be surprised how far I'm willing to go to make you happy." He teased between my thighs with his hard length, and my eyes rolled back in my head. "Tell me."

Forcing my brain to work, I mentally scanned the list for the easiest number available. A lightbulb clicked, and my eyes darted through the glass shower door to the huge mirror in my bathroom. I smiled timidly up at Rory as I stepped further under the water to rinse off, pulling him along with me. Shutting the water off, I handed him a towel as I dried myself off, but didn't bother putting clothes on.

He arched an eyebrow at me, and I motioned toward the mirror. He looked at our reflection in the glass and then back to me before it registered in his eyes. "Ah," he said, smirking as he dropped his towel. He licked his lips. "I love the way your mind works."

The heat in my cheeks doubled, but I held his gaze. He closed the distance between us, pushing some wet strands of my hair behind my ear.

"Turn around." He ordered and the dominant tone—so different from the soft and playful one he'd used seconds ago—awoke any senses that weren't already firing at full capacity.

I took a second too long to do what I was told, and he spun me around, so I faced the large mirror over my bathroom countertop. Heat blazed between my thighs as he pushed me from behind until my hips pressed against the marble. With one strong hand splayed across my back, he gave me a gentle nudge until I was leaning with my elbows on the cold surface. His knees brushed the back of my legs as he bent slightly over me, never losing my gaze in the mirror.

"I want you to watch me fuck you." His blue eyes were molten, and an ache wrenched itself low in my belly. He cupped my breasts as he kissed the back of my neck, down my spine, and back up again before he teased my wet center with the tip of his cock.

I gripped the countertop to keep from turning into a puddle but quickly moved to help guide him in, to put an end to his teasing.

He spun me back around, shaking his finger. "No. You watch."

His demand, paired with the full blasting light in the bathroom, turned up the intensity of the moment, though I didn't know how that was possible. The muscles in his abdomen flexed as he moved behind me and good *Lord* he was more glorious in this light than he had been in his loft. Nothing was hidden in the view in the mirror, and I couldn't help the wetness that slicked my thighs at the sight of his control over my body.

I tossed my hair over my shoulder, fully submitting to him as he rubbed his hands over my bare back. His thumbs worked over my hips, teasing with their proximity to my aching pussy. I arched my back, moving against his cock, trying to somehow draw it inside me without my hands.

Rory growled. "So fucking wet already."

I reached around and grabbed his hip, urging him closer. His wicked smirk had me wanting to spin around and demand he get inside me before I burst, but he quickly slid his free hand around me, stroking my clit with just enough pressure to make me buck backward against him.

"Rory," I begged.

"*Say it.*"

A thrill rushed through me, hot and pulsing. I knew from our night at his place what he needed—confirmation I wanted him as badly as possible.

"Fuck me already," I begged, knowing it turned him on that much more when I dropped the F-bomb.

He slammed inside me, all while keeping his fingers expertly massaging my clit, and the combination was perfection. I coiled inside, the pleasure hitting a crescendo as he thrust inside me over and over. I arched my head back and closed my eyes, my orgasm on the tip of his cock, but he froze.

"Eyes open, Red."

I snapped them open, locking onto to his molten-blue gaze in the mirror. "Watch me make you come."

Holy shit, the mouth on this man.

I clenched around him and bucked against his hand. I

couldn't help but notice how wild my own eyes were, or how delicious he looked behind me, inside me. He fit so well, rocking within me in the perfect rhythm. He relinquished control of my hip, grabbed my breast, and pinched my nipple at the same time as he did my clit with his other hand.

"Oh, God, Rory!" I gasped, the pleasure hitting me in a hard wave that crashed inside me, forcing trembles to wrack my body. He held me steady, his eyes locked onto mine in the mirror, watching me shake with ecstasy as he made good on his promise.

I sucked in a few deep breaths, recovering quickly as he continued to thrust. In a fast motion, I shoved him away enough for him to slip outside and for me to spin around. I hopped up onto the counter, bracing my hands on the edge for leverage.

"Your turn." I opened my legs, beckoning him back inside. He complied, the sweet motion of his reentry igniting all my already over-sensitive nerves again.

I locked my ankles around his waist and took control of the pace by squeezing my thighs around him. I rocked him in and out of me so hard, and so fast he didn't know what hit him—the shock evident in his wide, hot gaze which shifted from me to the mirror behind me.

His cock grew harder within my walls, and he gripped my ass, pumping against me to match my pace. That sweet pressure grew, spiraling low in my belly. A low growl escaped his mouth, and I moaned in response, another orgasm shaking my core as he came inside me.

I continued to ride him, working myself slowly down until I only slightly trembled against him. He pressed his forehead against my breasts, his hot breaths coming in ragged gasps against my skin.

Wrapping my arms around him, I held him to me, not wanting to let go, relishing the quiet moments after being so incredibly high. It didn't get any better than this. I knew that, now. Nothing would ever match how Rory could successfully push me to the edge; I just couldn't help but selfishly want him to crash over it with me.

CHAPTER 11

RORY

"FINALLY GET YOUR SHIT TOGETHER, old man?" Bentley—the rookie still vying for Gage's spot on the team—checked my shoulder as he skated passed me.

"Watch your mouth, kid. Wouldn't want to be forced to make an example out of you." I eyed him from under my helmet as we warmed up on the ice before the game. Today's game was important, and I wasn't letting that little shit in my head.

"Doubt that." The kid skated within an inch of my face. "In fact, it's been what? *Four* weeks since your last good brawl? I bet you're fucking *dying* for a fight."

Adrenaline surged in my blood, the old sensation I was much too familiar with—the one that ended fights, not started them. "You itching for a beating, Bentley? Didn't peg you for a submissive but hell, what you do off the ice is your own business." Gage skidded to a stop beside me. "Find someone else," I continued.

Bentley laughed. "That's right, I forgot. Your new chick put your balls on a keychain she keeps in her purse. Tell me, did she split them with Coach?"

I clenched my hand into a fist, ready to fly at him but the idea of the backlash for myself and Paige stopped me. Gage was in front of me before I could make a move, but it wasn't necessary. He tilted his head. "You good, bro?"

"Fuck yeah," I said, eyeing Bentley. "Little boy knows he can't fuck with you anymore. I'm the next best choice."

"Always second best," Gage joked, spinning toward Bentley. "Time to get off the ice, kid. The big boys are about to play."

I hissed, laughing as Bentley slowly skated backward toward the bench. "Damn, Rory. You used to be counted on for a good scrap. Now you're just as whipped as Gage." He spun and entered the box, shaking his head.

Keeping pace with Gage, we circled the ice, and I scanned the stands. "I'm not as whipped as you," I said.

"Keep telling yourself that." Gage bumped me with his shoulder. "Who you looking for again?"

I snapped my eyes back to him and the smug grin on his face. "Fuck you. I'm not."

"Uh huh."

The argument was right there and ready in my head, but it wasn't the truth. Even if I wanted to lie to myself, I couldn't. Paige had me completely wrapped around the same pretty polished finger she used to sign multi-million dollar deals. I was ready to do whatever she asked at the drop of a hat and found myself dying for the next item on her list.

After the night in her bathroom—where the hot as hell mirror action had taken me to an entirely new level of fucking—she'd slowly started letting me know more numbers she needed help crossing off. She'd told me number one last night, which was sex in public. I didn't have a clue how I was going to manage that one while also ensuring she didn't get caught—the press backlash would ruin her name, regardless if we were in a relationship or not —but I was damn sure going to make it happen.

A thought hit me as I finally spotted a mess of red hair in the stands—I liked her there. I liked the idea of her being there to watch *me*. And I liked the idea of her being mine. *Really* mine, not just a definition in a timed contract. Maybe Bentley wasn't far off the mark, despite his prick status. Maybe I was whipped.

Shit. When did that happen?

My best guess was somewhere between the balcony where she'd said she trusted me, to the bathroom where she submitted fully to my demands right before taking the reins and giving me the best orgasm of my life.

Fuck, head in the game.

I focused on the ice, on the opponents, and tuned out every other thought. There would be plenty of time for that shit later. Now I needed to show Coach that I was still Rory fucking Jackson.

Knowing she was up there watching me? I'd never played better.

We beat them in a shutout, and there wasn't a goon on the opposing team that wouldn't be sore tonight, not after what I'd done to them. It felt fucking great, too. At least on the ice, I could give in to the instincts that always bubbled near the surface with me and not catch shit for it—it's why I was the best enforcer the Sharks had. And with Paige's help, my nighttime brawls had been whittled down to zero. Turned out, when there was something at stake more important than just my ass, I could contain my short fuse just a little bit better. Or maybe it was because it *was* Paige that I gave a damn in the first place.

"Rory!" Coach shouted in the locker room, calling me

into his office. I scrubbed my freshly showered hair with a dry towel as I hovered in his doorway.

"Yeah?"

"You did good out there today."

"Thanks, Coach."

"You've been doing well off the ice too," he said, pointing to a picture he had up on his Mac on his desk. The shot was one of Paige and me outside the location for her future shelter—both covered in grime but grinning at each other like idiots. Thick bold lettering made up the headline:

Rory Jackson steals wholesome heart of Paige Turner.

Damn, we're really selling it.

I swallowed hard as Coach turned back toward me. "This change in you. Is it her?"

I nodded.

"I get that. There is something about a good woman who will turn us into the men we were always meant to be. And you were meant for more than bar brawls and bed-hopping."

Fuck, when did Coach become my father?

He cleared his throat. "Anyway. Keep it up."

"Will do, Coach." I turned to leave, but he called to stop me. I glanced at him over my shoulder.

"I'm proud of you," he said and then waved me off like I had knocked on his fucking door for the heart to heart.

"What are you laughing about?" Gage asked, slipping his duffle over his shoulder.

"Nothing, man." I tossed the now wet towel in an over-flowing hamper and tugged a white T over my head.

"Poker tonight?" He asked.

"I don't know," I said, grabbing my bag from my locker. "I'll have to check with Paige."

"See," Bentley blurted out beside us. "Fucking whipped."

Gage narrowed his eyes and whirled on him. "Dude, you're being like twenty times more annoying than usual. Did you just get dumped? Is that why you can't keep your mouth shut or are you simply hunting for pain?"

Bentley cowered in Gage's massive presence and held his hands up. "Whatever man. I'm out of here." He ducked his head and bolted out of the locker room.

"Oh shit, now I feel like an asshole," Gage said, shaking his head. "How'd the guy even get a girl let alone one long enough to dump him?"

I shrugged. "You can find anything on the internet these days." Gage laughed. "But I almost feel sorry for him," I continued. "I'd be a wreck if Paige left my ass out in the cold."

A shot of ice breezed through the center of my chest as the truth of my words caught up to me. I knew it was more than the contract we'd started with but the way I was acting, the way I was picturing a future together...fuck it was enough to freeze the blood in my veins. I'd never needed anyone in my life and a few weeks with Paige had turned me into...*Gage*. All lovestruck and moon-eyed and *fuck!*

I didn't even know if what I wanted was possible. Didn't know if I could dare to ask if Paige was feeling the heat like I was. Hell, I already knew I wasn't good enough for her, never would be. She needed to marry someone like a Kennedy, not a Shark.

Marry? Holy shit.

Could I be that guy? The one who woke up next to her every morning and slept with her every night. The one who attended charity galas with her on weeknights and served food in the shelter on the weekends. The life looked nothing like mine, but the more I pictured it, the more I pictured *her* in a constant place by my side, the more I wanted it.

But could she even contemplate a life married to *me?* Our contract was for three months for a reason. She was perfect for me, but damn if I wasn't a huge liability to her.

"Bro?" Gage smacked my chest, and I blinked out of my thoughts.

"What?" I snapped, unable to shake the knowledge that I was now picturing a future I knew I wasn't allowed to have.

"All right, it's a no on poker. Just double checking." He shook his head. "Don't let the rookie get under your skin, okay?"

I shook out my hands, which I only now realized I had clenched into fists. "I'm not."

Gage eyed me but let it go. He was good at not pushing when it wasn't needed. He fistbumped me before pushing out the door, and I heard the faintest squeal from Lettie as she saw her daddy.

That must be nice. I'd had the thought too many times and more than I'd ever admit to anyone—the thought that having a family waiting outside the door for you would be better than the puck bunnies that usually waited for me. *Used* to. Now I had Paige.

The knowledge that she was out there waiting for me shot a warmth through my chest that for once only half went to my dick.

I had Paige. For now. One month down. Two to go.

As I walked through the door I realized one crucial truth; three months would never be enough.

CHAPTER 12

PAIGE

I'D RESERVED a large table at *Nine's* for myself and three of the contractors who were currently working on my dream shelter, plus their lawyers and mine. I set the three iPads I'd brought with finalized terms and contracts on one, liability and insurance forms on the others. We'd agreed on prices after several weeks of back and forth on the plans until we finally reached a shared vision.

Jeannine had prepared my guests a special lunch menu of beef wellington and glazed carrots and paired it with their choosing of wine or liquor. The spread was to die for and half way through our meals my guests were *beyond* loose.

"We've had a variety of high-profile clients, Ms. Turner, but never one who is as particular as you are about every facet of this remodel." Mr. Langwater raised his glass of red in my direction, toasting with a smile and shake of his head.

I arched an eyebrow. "The design is critical to maintaining full-functionality and convenience for who I hire to run the shelter. It's vital we account for every need and *anticipated* need of the people who will be staying there.

This isn't about control, Mr. Langwater. It's about ensuring I produce the best possible product for those who will use it."

"Well said." He nodded, as did the others at the table, and I figured now was the perfect moment to get down to brass tacks.

I flipped open the iPads and drew up the documents on each screen, pushing them toward the men on the opposite side of the table. "As you can see here, everything we've discussed is in the contract. I will have paper copies sent to your offices as well if you'd like after we've each signed."

Mr. Langwater pulled out a pair of gold-rimmed reading glasses, and his partner and lawyers leaned in closer to look at each as well.

I made sure not to stare them down as they read over the fine print—though they were well-versed in the terms because I'd sent them a boilerplate contract last week. I glanced up as I took a sip of my water and caught two electric blue eyes that shook me to my core.

Rory raised his eyebrows from where he sat at the bar, completely inconspicuous in a cap, polo, and slacks combo. He could've been any man stopping for a drink after eighteen-holes, but *I'd* never overlook him. An urge to race across the restaurant and kiss him shot through my core. I held onto the table to steady myself as my heart raced. I couldn't be his version of Paige right now; I had my business face on.

But then he flashed me that damned smirk of his, the one that melted my insides while setting them on fire at the same time. He motioned behind him, where the hallway to the restrooms were.

I swallowed hard, noting the lawyers were still engrossed in the contracts. I scooted back from the table, drawing their attention. "Please excuse me, gentlemen. I'll give you a few moments in private to look over the paperwork."

"Of course." Mr. Langwater nodded and went back to reading.

It took everything in me not to sprint to the bathroom. A shock ran through me when I didn't find him waiting patiently outside them, and I froze in the hallway. I gasped, my brain catching up with the only reason he would've suggested I come this way. It wasn't to wait on him to take a piss before we chatted in hushed tones in a damned hallway. Nope. This was number one on my list, a number I'd told him about a few days ago.

I pushed through the lady's room door, my heart in my throat and my fingers trembling. My heels clicked against the tiled floor as I slowly walked to the only occupied stall. I pulled the door open, and Rory instantly yanked me inside, slamming and locking it behind me. He pressed me against the door, claiming my mouth with his, and I gasped between his lips. The first deep breath I'd taken all day came to me as his tongue slipped in my mouth.

Good God, I'd missed *him,* and it had only been a few days since I'd last seen him. I giggled against his lips, knocking his cap off his head. "What are we doing?" I asked, breathless and giddy.

He smirked, nibbling at my lower lip as his hands cupped my butt. "Number one plus number seven equals a fucking *ten.*"

I laughed again, then gasped as he sucked my tongue into his mouth. Adrenaline pulsed in my veins, shaking every inch of my body as the fear of getting caught mixed with the pure unshakable *need* I had for Rory. I shoved my hands under his shirt, needing to feel his skin under my fingertips. Knowing we didn't have a second to waste for me to get my nerves under control, I dove right in and unbuckled his belt and jerked his slacks down, pushing his abdomen until he fell backward and onto the closed lid of the toilet.

I didn't think about how I had a luncheon full of guests waiting for me to return or about how thankful I was that Jeannine didn't skimp on the luxury bathrooms—instead I hiked up my dress and shimmied my panties down, shocked the lacy thong didn't simply disintegrate the second his blue eyes had found mine.

Only breaking our kiss for a moment, I straddled him, rubbing my already wet center over his gorgeously hard cock.

"Fuck, *Red*," Rory hissed, gripping my hips as he looked up at me. "I missed you."

A tiny moan escaped my lips, the only intelligible response I had for him when he was teasing me.

"Me too." I drug the words out, shamelessly rocking forward and back against him, teasing him as much as he did me.

His fingers clutched my hips, picking up my pace and then slowing it down. I ached, but with each attempt to get him inside me, he prevented it.

"Rory, please don't do this to me." I dug my nails into his shoulder and pressed my breasts into his chest.

He sucked my lip into his mouth before grinning at me deviously. "You might want to keep it down, Red. Never know who could walk in at any moment."

I gasped as he hefted me against him, his hard cock pressing against my clit before he moved me away again. I clamped my mouth shut; the concentration took an effort I'd never experienced before.

Rory went silent, too, but pinned me with his gaze and the motions of his hands. He knew just how to move me, just where to angle me to wind me up, and then when I was sure I'd come from the pressure he had on my clit alone, he'd release it, and I'd come down—wetter and more frustrated than I knew possible.

His eyes darkened at another failed attempt by me to get him inside, and I tilted my head back, sucking in slow breaths that if we were not in a public bathroom would be begging screams.

His strong hand at the back of my neck had me face to face with him, and he licked his lips, the blue in his eyes sparking. He kissed me instead of giving in to my silent demands, and while it was hot as hell, I wanted *more*.

Finally, I fought the guidance of his teasing hands. I forced myself to freeze, unable to take the torture for one more second. Still, the feel of his hard cock simply *being* under me was enough to make me pulse.

Rory tightened his grip on my hips and tried to move me, but I shook my head. "Please, I can't take anymore."

He kissed my neck, my collarbone, and trailed his tongue along the shell of my ear before trying to move me again. "God, you smell like bottled sunshine. I'll never get enough of this—of you," he said as I resisted, my thighs trembling from the strain. He gave me a light smack on my butt, just enough to sting, and I bucked against him. His cock plunged inside me, the friction so sweet I almost instantly came. I rocked against him, hard and fast, meeting each one of his pumps as they came. I took him in. Took as much as he'd give me.

The throbbing knots within me tightened to an all-time high before Rory gave one final thrust and sent me over the edge again, forcing me to fly apart in his arms. He held me close as I came so hard I shook against him, and he swallowed my moans with his mouth claiming mine.

After a few moments of collecting our breath, he smoothed my hair over my face. The look in his eyes was so open and genuine—or maybe it was just the high from the cosmic orgasm he'd just delivered me—but I couldn't hold my tongue back a second longer, not with what he'd just said to me. Sure, maybe it was the heat of passion, but he'd said *never get enough.*

"I want this to be real, Rory." I blurted the words out as if I was a champagne bottle and he had just popped my verbal cork.

His eyes widened, the crease I knew all too well forming between his eyes

"I know I shouldn't," I whispered, my eyes dropping to his chest.

He tilted my chin up, a smile tugging at the corners of his lips before he kissed me gently. "This is as real as it gets, Red."

The breath stalled in my lungs as his eyes searched mine. "Truly?"

He nodded. "You don't need a fucking contract to tell you I'm yours. I have been since the night I took you to my loft. Maybe before that."

Tears bit the backs of my eyes, but I locked it up and kissed him frantically. After a few blissful moments where my heart soared with all the things I never thought I'd get to have, the fear of the stakes that came with a relationship like ours battled the happiness filling my heart.

I rose off of him as gently as I could, and the second my heels clicked on the tiled floor, reality crashed on top of me. The luncheon. My contractors! Good Lord, Rory was capable of making me forget *everything.*

I straightened myself, pulling my panties up only to have Rory's hand dart out before I got them all the way up. He stroked me for a few seconds, just enough to properly rile me up again and to soak his hand in the scent of us. After he pulled it back, he inhaled long and deep.

Oh God, if I didn't go right this minute, I'd have him on *this* bathroom counter.

"I'm sorry to rush out..."

"Don't be. Go." He grinned, motioning toward the door.

I turned and opened it, checking the mirror to make sure I didn't look too *just-been-fucked* and was satisfied only my flushed skin gave me away. I glanced back in the mirror, noticing a playful smirk shaped Rory's lips.

I washed my hands quickly and darted out the door and back to my table.

Mr. Langwater and his partners had set the iPads down and were selecting samples off of dessert trays that Jeannine had prepared for the lunch. *Thank God for chocolate and Jeannine.*

"I apologize, gentlemen. I'm close with the owner and got caught up in a chat." The lie was rough coming out, and I prayed Jeannine hadn't personally delivered the tray of sweets or I'd look like an asshole.

"I wish I had friends like you do." Mr. Langwater popped a chocolate truffle in his mouth and pushed the still-opened iPads toward me and my two lawyers that had joined in on the dessert fest. "We've signed. Everything is in perfect working order, as we expected no less. You truly are a remarkable business woman, Ms. Turner."

I smiled as I scooped up the iPads, signing the portions left blank for my signature with the stylus. "Thank you, Mr. Langwater. I'm thrilled to be working with a firm as prestigious as your own. I know you'll make this dream of mine a reality." I instantly emailed a copy of the contracts and forms to his office as soon as I'd signed, slightly mystified I could close a big-business deal right after Rory had made me come in the bathroom minutes ago. My cheeks flushed at the thought, and I shifted in my seat.

"Now that they're signed, do we have to rush off? I'd really love to try as many of these marvelous desserts until I'm incapable of eating more." Mr. Langwater smiled and reached for another truffle.

"Of course. I can always have Jeannine bring more if you feel up to the challenge."

He laughed and waved his hands in defeat. "No, no no. I couldn't possibly."

I chuckled and took a much needed pull from my ice water, letting the cool liquid quench a thirst only Rory managed to create. I casually glanced around the restaurant as the men chatted amongst themselves between bites of chocolate, hunting for a pair of blue eyes that had the ability to see into my soul.

I found him by the door, readying to leave. He winked at me as he pressed his fingers against his lips. The fingers that I knew were enveloped in the scent unique to the two of us together, and a warm chill raked over my skin. He'd said what we had was real. He'd felt what I did. Maybe not love, but he was with me. And he was *mine*.

Another moment and he turned out of the door, leaving me with a pleasant ache between my thighs and a raw craving for more.

I hit up the local boutiques after the luncheon. A celebration/distraction trip that doubled as a time-killer until Jeannine closed up. After she'd locked the doors well after midnight, she poured us both drinks, and we sat at the bar.

"You did *what* in my bathroom?" She nearly spit out her club soda after I'd quickly confessed my sin of the day. She wiped her mouth with the back of her hand.

"I'm sorry?" I downed a gulp of scotch and soda.

She waved me off. "It's already cleaned up by now."

I laughed. "God, Jeannine we didn't make a mess."

"Sure, sure. You know I spent over a hundred grand on those bathrooms and you go and get your ladybits all over—"

"Jeannine!" I held my side from laughing so hard, her joining in as she shook her head.

"It's all right. That's another one off the list right?"

I nodded, unable to contain my smile.

"You've got it bad."

"I'm afraid I do." I took another gulp and turned to face her. "Now, tell me all the consequences of giving my heart to a notorious bad boy Shark. Tell me the risk of loving someone who is capable of ruining my public persona. Tell me all of it, Nine, because I've kept the thoughts at bay all day and now they're consuming me."

"Whoa," Jeannine said, pouring me another drink and sliding it in front of me. "First, drink some more. Then take a damn breath."

I obeyed, drinking and breathing and trying to shove every reason I knew I shouldn't be with Rory in a box labeled *save for later*.

Jeannine studied me with weary eyes. "You said love."

I nodded. "I don't know if he loves me. I know that we have something...maybe I'm crazy." I pinched the bridge of my nose.

"Don't belittle it," she said. "You two have some serious chemistry working. Anyone can see it."

"And that's the problem, isn't it? People who can see. Sure we're doing okay in the media's eyes now, but what if he slips? What if he gets arrested again? What if he goes back to bed-hopping and I'm left looking like the idiot girl who was swept away by a Shark?"

"He's not stupid enough to do any of those things."

"I hope you're right, but my head..." I smacked my palm against my forehead. "My damn business head is telling me to run away now before I fall worse."

"I know you're required to think like that, but *seriously*? How can you turn your back on something like the two of you have? If I had a man who could distract me enough to make me forget I was in a restaurant bathroom, let alone a *meeting*? I'd put a death-grip *and* a ring on it."

I laughed and finished the contents of my drink.

"What does your heart say?" Jeannine asked.

"That I'm in love with him." I rested my forehead on the bar. "But he drives me insane."

"I can see that."

I tossed my head up. "No, you don't get it. He makes me think terrible things."

She arched an eyebrow at me. "Like what?"

I polished off my scotch. "Like maybe I don't care what happens if I lose everything else, as long as I have him."

She hissed and poured me another. "That's the dirty-girl in you talking, and I'm beyond glad the list and Rory has brought her out in you, but you've got to find the balance between the brilliant woman you are—and all the responsi-bilities that go with her—and the girl who needs to cross off everything on that list."

"I don't care about the list anymore. I care about being out of control of my own choices."

"You're in control, Paige. You always are. You just need

to figure out a way to manage both." She placed her hand on my back.

"What if I can't? What if the *only* thing I manage is to fuck everything up."

Jeannine raised her glass to mine and clinked the rim. "You won't." After a good, long drink she set her glass on the bar and leaned on her elbows to get close to me. "But if you do I'm always hiring."

I chuckled and rubbed my palms over my face. They still smelled like Rory's skin and the ever-present craving for his presence wrenched in my core. I silenced it with a prayer that I could find the balance Jeannine spoke of. Find a way to be the woman the world and my company needed me to be, and the woman who loved Rory Jackson with her whole heart. Now I had to hope he wouldn't crush it.

CHAPTER 13

RORY

"ONE MORE TIME, UNCLE RORY!" Lettie squealed as I pushed her on the swing on the fort I'd help Gage build for her fourth birthday. I sucked in a deep breath, ignoring the stitch in my side. Forget grueling hockey practices, Lettie could outlast Coach and half the Sharks on the team.

I held up my finger, exaggerating my need for oxygen a little for theatrics. "One. More. Time."

She giggled, her cute little smile stretching across her tiny face as she wiggled in the seat of the swing.

"Hang on tight," I whispered as I pulled the swing back slowly, dragging out the anticipation before letting her fly.

Her delighted scream filled the backyard and was infectious enough to have me laughing too.

"Ready to crank out a kid?" Gage asked, handing me a beer as he returned from his trip to the cooler on the back patio.

I took a hard gulp, unable to answer with one of my usual quick quips.

"Shit," Gage said, laughing as he shook his head.

"What?" I tried to rally. "No man can be around Lettie for more than an hour and *not* want kids."

He smacked my back with his free hand and leaned against the wooden fort as Lettie took off at breakneck speed to zoom down the slide a hundred times in a row. Or at least that is what it looked like.

"She's my world." Gage had that faraway look in his eyes, the one that only showed up if Lettie or Bailey were in the room.

I chugged another swallow, my grip tightening around the bottle. "This family stuff," I said, motioning with my bottle to Lettie and then toward Bailey where we could just barely see her through the kitchen window. "Is it all it's cracked up to be?"

He shifted, pushing off the fort to stand in front of me. "Rory Jackson," he said my name like he'd just put together a puzzle. "It *finally* happened."

I rolled my eyes. "Eat shit."

Gage laughed. "You're in love."

My nostrils flared as I struggled to breathe—for real this time. "What if I was?"

He shrugged. "There isn't a better woman out there, except for my Bailey of course. And they've been friends for years. Paige is smart, sexy, and just about the only woman I've ever seen lengthen that short fuse of yours. I'm shocked it's taken you this long to realize it."

I snorted, finishing off my beer. He wasn't wrong, but I couldn't shake the cold eating away at my gut.

"What's up?" Gage pressed me when I didn't respond.

I shook my head, spinning the empty bottle in my hand. "I don't want to fuck it up," I admitted, finally looking him in the eye. He was the closest I'd ever had to a brother, and I knew he'd give it to me straight. "I don't know if I'm cut out for this life." I gestured to the area around us—Gage's perfect house, with his perfect daughter, and perfect fiancé carrying yet another perfect child in her belly.

"Please, you're amazing with Lettie." He scoffed.

"That's because she's Lettie. And besides, I'm not there yet." I shifted my weight. "Paige is unlike any woman I've ever been with. Add to that the insane heat her company puts on her for every little thing she does? I could easily ruin things for her. My temper..." The breath stalled in my lungs, the thought of things going south because I couldn't control the rage that lived inside my veins had my chest tightening.

"Have you talked to her about..." Gage hesitated until he caught my eye. "You know?"

I shook my head. "Not yet. Figured I'd better wait another month or so before I drop the bomb on her. No one wants to know about an abusive childhood only a month into a new relationship." That and I honestly didn't want her to know I had a monster's blood in my veins—that my father was the source for the instant fight trigger I possessed.

Gage winced but nodded. He was the only other person I'd ever told about my past, about why I was always ready to finish a fight if someone even breathed on me the wrong way. It was how I'd had to live for years under my father's rule, and it was the only way I'd known how to live after I escaped him at sixteen. I left home and never looked back. Fuck, my mother had helped me pack. She'd believed *I* was the cause of his anger, that I brought it out in him instead of there being something internally wrong with him.

"Anyway," I said, shaking out my limbs that had clenched on their own. Shit, it'd been years, and the thought of the past still had the ability to pump adrenaline through my veins as if I were five and helpless again. I may have cut all family ties, but I'd carried the need to never feel weak around with me as a constant reminder of who I'd never allow myself to be again. "I don't want who I am to ruin who she is."

"Can't you ever give yourself some credit, man?" Gage took a drink of his beer. "I mean, look at you. It's only been a month with her, and you're playing better, on and off the ice. I've never seen you happier, or more with your shit together."

I nodded. Even coach had noticed, and I couldn't deny I liked the way my life felt with her in it—complete, hopeful, hot as hell. "Honestly, man. Do you think I stand a chance? I can't see clearly. Paige is clouding up my mind with dreams of a future I may not deserve." I looked him in the eye, needing to see the absolute truth from him. "Tell me to stay away from her. Tell me to stop this before I get in too deep and taint her perfect image."

"I can't," he said, clamping his hand on my shoulder. "She's too good for you, sure. But so is Bailey for me. It doesn't matter. You love her?" He eyed me, needing the confirmation.

"Fuck, yeah man. I love her." I nearly choked on the sweet words, but they were there, and once spoken, hardened into the kind of foundation I could build on with Paige. A real life. A real family. A real future.

He nodded, like that was the answer to every doubt I had. "Good. Remember that. Whenever you feel yourself slipping into that old *punch first ask questions later* feeling—off the ice at least—remember that. Use her to put a lock on that lifestyle for good. You'll be better off for it, happier too."

I released a breath I hadn't realized I'd been holding

and pressed my lips together as I smacked the arm on my shoulder. "Thanks, bro. I needed that."

"Should we hug this shit out?" Gage laughed, reaching out to me like a giant bear going in for the bone-crushing attack.

"Hell no!" I ducked out of his would-be embrace, chuckling as Lettie opted to turn it into a game, running from her daddy the bear. She'd just saved me from sudden death when my cell buzzed in my pocket. I took a quick time out to read the text.

COACH: *You have ten minutes to get to my office. I don't give a shit where you're at.*

COACH: *TEN. MINUTES.*

"Ah what the fu—" I stopped myself short as I drew my eyes back up, noticing Lettie only a foot away from me as she hung off Gage's neck like a monkey.

"What's up?" He asked.

I scrunched my eyebrows and shrugged. "Coach. He's pissed, but I haven't got a clue what about."

Gage cocked an eyebrow at me.

"What?" I asked innocently. "I've been a good little boy."

"Anything before this past month that could've had a delayed release?"

My eyes glazed over as I tried to think that far back, it felt like a year had passed not a month. Paige had shaken up my world enough to fuck with time now. "I don't think so?" I honestly didn't have a clue but rushed up to Lettie and planted a quick kiss on her cheek. "Thanks for the talk," I said to Gage as I hurried toward his house.

"You going to grab that ratchet set on your way out?" Gage called just as I made it to his back door.

I turned around and shook my head, nearly forgetting

that was the excuse I'd given him when I'd showed up unannounced at his door. He knew it was bullshit.

"Next time." I ducked inside and stormed out his front door with a muttered apology to Bailey.

I took the highway, speeding well over the limit toward the rink. I'd just gotten off of Coach's shit-list and wouldn't give him another excuse to put me back on it.

Sprinting into the building and through the locker room, I made it with about twenty seconds to spare. Flushed and out of breath, I knocked on his opened door.

"Coach?"

He spun around in his chair, the purple vein in his forehead already puckered and throbbing.

Fuck my life. What had I done?

"Sit." He motioned to the chair across from his desk, and I sank into it.

"What is going on?" I blurted out, unable to keep my mouth shut. I'd busted my ass at practices, killed it in games, and had steered clear of the bars for a month now. I shouldn't be getting these kind of texts from Coach, damn it.

He rested his elbows on the desk, threading his fingers together as he took a long, deep breath. "You remember when I told you I was proud of you?"

Acid bubbled up in my throat, and I swallowed it down. "Yes, sir."

"Did you think that was code for go off the rails again?"

"What? No. Of course not."

"When I said Ms. Turner was good for you, did you think I meant *she's good for you why don't you rake her through the coals, publically?*"

"Excuse me for saying this, sir, but what in the absolute hell is going on?"

Coach huffed, unimpressed by my complete oblivious-ness to whatever the situation was. He spun his monitor around, showing me the photograph that took up half of his large screen. I squinted at the shot, my mind quickly trying to rationalize when it had been taken.

Linda had her arms wrapped around my neck, my hands on her hips as I looked down at her outside the rink.

"Fuck!" I snapped, instantly clenching my jaw. Next to that picture was one of Paige, alone as she wiped tears from her eyes. It was a close-up shot as if the paps had zoomed in on her face, but I recognized the collar of the T-shirt she had —mostly because I remembered peeling it off her after a long, hard day of working at her site.

The headline suggested I was a cheating bastard who had broken Paige's heart and now her emotional stability and well-being was in question.

"This is bullshit, Coach." I jerked my hand toward the images.

"Is it?" He snapped. "There are ten more sites running the same images. Each one has a different story. Some are saying she stole you from the other one, labeling her as an adulterator."

"It's not true!" I bolted out of my seat, the adrenaline raging in my blood too much to take sitting. "That shot was taken months ago. Before Paige and I even..." Saying her name was like a reminder to take a deep fucking breath, so I did.

He examined me through narrowed eyes but eventually sighed.

"I believe you," Coach finally said, eyeing the seat. I sat back down, each one of my muscles locked and tense. "But this is exactly the kind of shitstorm we don't need. We have an actual shot at the Championship this season, and a media war with a company like CranBaby won't help you keep your head in the game."

"Coach, I promise you this has no grounds. Paige and I...well, I *love* her." Shit might as well make a fucking announcement on the hottest gossip blog for how many people I was spouting my feelings too. Maybe it would help squash this shit. "I would never do anything to hurt her. Especially something like that." I pointed to the screen again, and he turned it back toward him. "It's the damn paps. They're out for blood."

"Aren't they always?" Coach rubbed his forehead, closing his eyes. "I had to see your reaction, son. That's why I called you over here so quickly. I believe you. I can see it in your eyes you love this girl." He finally looked up at me. "But can I offer some advice?"

"Please."

"Lay low. The both of you. Stay out of public for a while, give the bloodhounds time to get bored and hunt for someone else."

I nodded, wishing like hell I could track down the pap who'd snapped that shot of Linda and me. I fucking remembered the day. I'd been pushing Linda away, not pulling her closer. Fucking reporters.

"Is Paige handling this all right?" Coach asked, and I snapped my head up, my eyes popping wide. I stood up, my mouth hanging open. Had she seen it yet? Had her father?

"I have to go." I turned toward the door before stopping. "I mean, am I...is it okay if I—"

"Go," Coach cut me off. "Be honest with her. Make sure she knows the truth."

"Right," I said and bolted out the door. Seemed like all I was doing today was running. Only now I was headed toward a storm I didn't know I'd survive. If Paige didn't believe me—believe that picture was months old—then I'd lose her.

Ice cold fear clung to my gut as I sank behind the wheel of my SUV. I'd only just now realized I loved her and I wasn't about to let anyone fuck it up for me.

CHAPTER 14

PAIGE

"EXPLAIN." My father slapped a thin magazine down on my desk, the force of the action making me jump.

The cover of the magazine completely overshadowed the proposal outlined I'd been reading before he'd burst in. I studied the picture for several moments and re-read the headline and subtext four times.

Busty-VP of Cranbaby Organics, Paige Turner, steals bad-boy enforcer for the Seattle Sharks, Rory Jackson, from his widely rumored girlfriend, Linda Wallace, who has been a permanent seat warmer at the Shark's stadium for the past two seasons. Perhaps this well-known-do-gooder isn't as innocent as we all are meant to believe.

The words were laid above a picture of Rory gripping the hips of a blonde bunny I'd seen more times than I could count outside the Sharks' locker room. A crack opened up in my chest just enough to sear. *He'd said we were real.* And before that, he'd signed a damn contract assuring me exclusivity.

Notorious player. Bed-hopping bad-boy. The names the media had often used to describe him flashed in my mind, each time filling my head with more and more doubt. *Was he playing me?*

"Well?" My father snapped before I could gather my thoughts enough to make a decision. He loosened the tie around his neck, and I put a lock on the tears threatening to escape my eyes. Now was not the time to show emotion. Not here. Not at work. In front of my father/boss.

"This picture could've been taken at any time before we met," I said, rising from my seated position to match his stance. "He wasn't attached when we started dating." The emphasis I put behind my words was almost enough to convince my heart, but a history of Rory's promiscuity had doubt seeping through every crack I had in the wall around my heart. The same heart that Rory had recently branded his fucking name on. "She could be a friend," I added as I glanced down at the picture again.

Father rolled his eyes. "The article suggests a hell of a lot more than friendship, Paige. The other woman is quoted as *heartbroken*." He paced in front of my desk.

My chest tightened at the words. Shit. "This is what the paparazzi do. Twist things. Rory wouldn't do this—"

"He *would*! That's who he is." He pinched the bridge of his nose. "This is exactly the reason I told you to stay away from him."

"What? You told me I was a grown woman capable of making my own choices!" I was thankful for the desk between us because I had the urge to strangle him.

"Clearly I thought you were smart enough to make the *right* decisions."

"You mean the decisions *you'd* make for me."

He tossed his hands in the air. "Well, what would you have me think? Our public relations team has gotten over thirty calls about the situation, not even mentioning the angry consumer emails we've received, and this only released this morning! I won't even discuss the forums on the blog because they're downright malicious."

I shook my head and pressed the intercom on my desk. "Get me, Kelsey. Quickly, please."

"Right away, Ms. Turner." I took my hand off the intercom and looked my father in the eye.

"I will handle this."

"You have to. Regardless of the legitimacy of these claims we are now suffering a backlash. I'd suggest you issue a public statement as soon as possible." He lowered his voice to the tone he reserved for getting his way in any sort of deal. "A statement denying real romantic ties to Rory Jackson would be the best avenue to take."

I gaped at him for a moment before I shoved my cell in my purse. Kelsey walked through the door, saving me from going off on my own father. I motioned to the seat behind my desk, her eyes darting between my father and me as she sat down. "I need you to filter directions on all our social media sites—post my statement and run interference. Try to cool the heat hitting us." I slipped my purse over my shoulder and walked around my desk.

"Of course." Kelsey didn't need to ask what about, yet another reason why I'd kept her for so many years—she was on top of everything, always. "What *is* your statement, Paige?" She held a pen over a scratch notebook I kept in my desk drawer.

I clenched my eyes shut for a moment preparing myself for the awful sensation of deliberately disappointing my father—it was sour and heavy in my stomach—but I couldn't lie. Whether it was anyone's business or not what I did in my personal life, I wouldn't publically strip myself of Rory... not without hearing his side of the story first.

One crisis at a time.

I opened my eyes, locking onto my father's but speaking to her. "Rory Jackson and I are in a happy, healthy relationship. The accusations of the articles are under investigation by my team, and I sincerely apologize to anyone the misunderstanding may have hurt in any way, including the referenced Ms. Linda Wallace."

Kelsey nodded as she wrote down each word before looking up at me. "Anything else?"

"Yes. Track down the reporter who penned the article. The picture is real, but the words behind it are borderline liable. We need to see who he spoke with, if anyone, and why they'd want to sabotage Rory and me."

Dad crossed his arms over his chest, the frustration in his eyes slowly ebbing with each firm action I took. "Rory will agree with your statement if they ask him for comment, correct?"

I swallowed past the lump in my throat. I had no idea what Rory's reaction to this would be. If he'd lied to me and had been "cheating" on me the entire time, he might say anything to the papers.

He wouldn't do this. You know he wouldn't.

The reassuring voice in the back of my head was growing smaller the longer I stood in my office, unsure and analyzing every encounter between Rory and myself for the past month. Had I been falling for him while he'd kept true to his playboy ways? Had everything he'd said, done, just been part of the role I'd hired him to play? Had he only been mine on the days we'd seen each other?

"Paige?" My father snapped me out of my thoughts, his tone soft for the first time since he entered my office.

"He wouldn't do this. You don't know him." Dad's eyes

slowly closed as I walked out of my office and toward the elevator. I typed out a fast text to Rory.

ME: *Meet me?*

Rory instantly texted back: *Anywhere.*

ME: *Leaving office. Closer to your place.*

RORY: *Halfway there.*

I leaned my head back against the elevator, trying to calm my racing heart as I took the long ride down. At least he was willing to meet me. That gave what little hope that clung to my heart enough spark to breathe.

After a short drive and another elevator ride up, my hands shook as I reached up to knock on his front door. My knuckles didn't get within an inch of it before Rory was there, jerking me into the loft with a frantic look in his eyes.

"It's not true," he said, his voice rushed as if he'd ran the whole way home from the rink.

The tears I'd held back since my father burst into my office filled my eyes. I was useless in Rory's presence—I heard his voice, and it instantly stripped me of my strongest defenses.

"Promise me?" I demanded, but it came out sounding more like a question.

Rory timidly wrapped his arms around my waist, sliding his hands slowly across my back. "I promise, Red. I haven't touched another woman since that night at the Four Seasons. How could I even think about another woman if I have you? Hell, even the possibility of having you was enough to keep away from anyone else."

My heart flipped in my chest, the sincerity in his eyes shining through the swirling blues. "And Linda?"

He hissed, his hold on me tightening a fraction. "She's a bunny."

"Yours?"

"No," he snapped before tilting his head. "Once." He squinted in apology. "Okay, twice. But it was a year ago."

I pressed my lips together, knowing about his past and having it slap me in the face were two very different things. "The picture?"

"A week before the Four Seasons." I tried to tug out of his grasp, needing the room to breathe, but he held me close. "I was pushing her away. Telling her off. I've had to do it more than once. She won't take the hint."

I stopped pulling against him, the business side of my brain clicking on. "She's the one who gave the reporter the picture and the details."

"You think?"

"Who else would gain from this mess?" I shook my head, the anger stealing the tears away. *Damn, I'm an emotional, hot mess. Is this what love does to a person?*

"Fuck," he snapped and released me. His fists clenched at his sides as he paced back and forth. "You believe me, don't you?" The anger in his voice was mounting in a way I hadn't heard before.

I cupped his cheek with my hand, stopping his movements. He was shaking again. "I do." I forced him to look at me. "Rory. Breathe."

He closed his eyes and sighed as he pressed his forehead against mine. "I love you." I froze in his embrace, my heart soaring at his words and choking my airways. He kept his eyes firmly shut as he hurried on. "And I know I'm a selfish asshole for saying it. You're so much better off without me." He huffed. "Can you feel me, now? This rage? It's in my blood, Red. It'll always be there no matter what, just waiting for the perfect moment to seep out and ruin everything you hold dear."

I swallowed hard. "Why are you so hard on yourself?"

He slowly he peeled his eyes open, locking them with mine. "It's in my *blood*. Anger. Rage. My father, he..." Rory's eyes shot to the floor as he gripped my hands in his. "His idea of welcoming me home from school was a beat down. For reasons I never understood. I only ever knew I was helpless against him. Weak. My mother blamed me. Said there was something in me that brought it out in him. That he'd been perfect before she'd brought me into the world. I left home the minute I could. I never knew what having a real family looked like, *felt* like until I met Gage." He sucked in a deep breath as tears rolled down my cheeks. He glanced back up at me. "And now you. I didn't think it was possible to want or love anyone as much as I love you, Red. But with who I am...what I can't help but be...I know I shouldn't be allowed to have someone as amazing as—"

I cut his words off with a crushing kiss as if I could force all the doubts he had about himself away with the pressure of my lips. After a few moments, I pulled back, shaking my head slightly as I pushed away some blond hair that had fallen in his eyes. "You're not him, Rory. You're a great man. If you weren't...I wouldn't love you as much as I do." I said the last words as boldly and clearly as I could, not wanting him to doubt for one more second.

"Fuck, you do?" He chuckled. "Really?"

"Truly."

He lifted me off the ground, bringing me to his eye level as he claimed my mouth. Heat unfurled in my core as his tongue stroked the edges of my teeth, successfully stealing my already erratic breath. Without moving to put me back on my feet, he pulled away just enough to look at me.

"I'm sorry it all came out this way."

I tilted my head.

"I wanted to tell you...I don't know, over a romantic dinner or something. Not in response to an external threat."

I had completely forgotten Linda and the picture and what had brought this all on. "I don't care how you came to say it," I said, planting a soft kiss on his lips. "I'm just glad you did."

"You're the perfect woman."

"No. Neither of us is perfect. We're both jagged in different places. We just *fit*." And now that I knew he felt the same way, everything else in comparison seemed small and so far away. Linda, the reporters, his dark past, my impending takeover of the company—I could handle it all with Rory at my side.

A smirk shaped his lips, the blue of his eyes turning molten. The look was enough to melt my panties. "What are you thinking?"

"You're here. We're in love. Let's do something dirty."

I laughed, loving that he was capable of making me feel light as air on a day that had been more than heavy. "Pick a number between one and twelve."

"Two," he instantly said.

I clenched my eyes shut. "You *would*." I shook my head. "Two is the one thing on the list I absolutely can't do. Not now."

"Not now what?"

"That I love you."

"And before?"

"The idea was entertained with the help of Jeannine, Bailey, and a great deal of margaritas."

He chuckled, the hard planes of his chest vibrating underneath me. "What is it?"

Heat flushed my cheeks. "Have a threesome." His eyes

popped wide, and I arched an eyebrow at him. "*Not* going to happen."

He licked his lips, playfully teasing my lower lip. "You think I'd ever share you, Red?" After a moment he set me gently on my feet. "Come with me."

"Where?" I asked as he pulled me toward his front door.

He paused when he opened it. "Do you trust me?"

A warm shiver danced across my skin just as it had when he'd first asked me. "Yes."

"Then you'll see." He intertwined our fingers and guided me out the door.

After fifteen minutes of being kissed senseless outside Rory's building, a black Cadillac Escalade pulled in front of us. Its headlights exposed the way our bodies were practically melded together, and I quickly put distance between us as if my parents had just walked in on me making out in my room.

"Dave has been my driver for years," Rory said and opened the door to the third row of seats, deliberately putting a row of space between the driver and us.

"You always sit back here?" I slid in and buckled my seatbelt. *What was he up to?*

"It's the best seat for us tonight."

A rush of adrenaline soared through my blood as I gauged the distance between us and Dave the driver. There was no illusion of privacy except for the fact that he kept his eyes firmly planted in front of him.

"Oh my God," I whispered, registering the devious glint in Rory's eyes. "You're not serious."

Rory shifted to get closer to me. "You *hired* me to help you check off items on your list. I'm nothing if I don't do my duty." He teased me, slipping his tongue between my lips for a brief second before pulling back. The challenge was clear in his eyes, almost as clear as the hesitance as he waited to see if I took the bait or not.

"Dave," I spoke up and found it incredible that he didn't glance in his rearview to look me in the eye. "Will you drive us to my house please?" I rattled off the address though I knew he'd dropped Rory off before. The distance between our places would be just enough time.

"Yes, Ma'am," Dave replied.

I turned my attention back to Rory who gazed at me with a shocked look. "You started this," I reminded him with a wicked grin. I slipped my hand underneath his shirt, relishing the feel of his hard abs and smooth skin. Working lower, I managed to get my hand beneath the waist of his jeans. He was already on his way to a raging hard on, and my thighs clenched at the idea of him getting off with simple touches from me.

Unbuckling my seatbelt, I scooted toward him until I could straddle his lap.

"Paige," He groaned, looking over my shoulder. "Wait. I didn't think this one through. It isn't exactly *safe.*"

I tilted my head and re-plunged my hand down his pants. "That's sweet. The good man in you worrying about me, but I'd like to speak with my bad boy, now, please."

He nipped at my bottom lip.

"Unless he's checked out of the game?" I stopped the stroking of his now fully hard cock.

Rory ran his hands up my thighs nestled on either side of him, sliding my dress up until it flared around his lap. "Oh, he's here. Right. Here." He accentuated the word with his fingers pressing expertly against my clit.

I hissed and moved my hips against his touch, the motion placing my breasts at the perfect angle for his mouth. He kissed the modest cleavage that my very innocent gray dress showed, and I leaned my lips to his ear. "We've got fifteen minutes before we reach my house. You think I can make you come before then?"

His eyes locked with mine. "Have I ever lost a challenge?"

"This will take number eight off the list right alongside number two." Anticipation flared in my chest with the challenge. "And nothing is impossible, Rory." *Hell, the notorious player had fallen for me.* And I had fallen right back.

I withdrew my hand long enough to unbutton and unzip his jeans, and he shifted in his seat to wiggle them down slightly. I then pushed his hand away from working over my clit, instantly missing the pressure, but needing *more.*

His breath hitched as his eyes followed my hand, touching myself beneath my panties, coating my fingers in my warmth. I reclaimed his cock with my properly slicked hand, massaging it with a gliding ease. He groaned and arched his head back as I strengthened my grip, picking up the pace of my strokes.

"Try not to scream," I whispered in his ear. "Don't want to distract the third person in this ménage, *your* driver." I glanced over my shoulder, finding Dave's eyes still dutifully on the road. I enjoyed the power I had over Rory in the moment. The fact that I held him in pleasure-filled agony not ten feet from his driver. It was my turn to get him off in a place he least expected it—and since he said it would never happen, I only wanted to do it more.

He pulled on my hips in an attempt to settle my wetness over him, but I resisted, shaking my head. "Not yet," I said and circled the tip of his cock with my thumb.

"Damn it, Red. Your scent. It's all over me. I want it in my mouth."

I contemplated the acrobatics of that request before dismissing it. The act of which, again, only seemed to turn him on more. I held on strong despite his thrusts against my hand and his near primal need to get inside me making my already steaming thighs hotter.

"How bad do you want it?" I asked against his lips, turning the tables on him. How many times had Rory made me speak my needs before he'd made me fly apart?

He jerked down on my hips but remained silent.

I circled the outside of my center with his tip, rewetting it. I was rewarded with a gentle bite on my lip.

"Say it, Rory. Or I will end it." I demanded the words from him as he had me so many times already. The surge of control went straight to my head, and the tension low in my belly tightened, twisted, and knotted.

"Paige—" He groaned. "Now."

Good enough for me. I released his cock and wrapped my arm around his neck. He plunged inside me as I bucked against him. He growled so loud I shoved my hand over his mouth, silencing him. The action made him thrust harder, and I clenched around him, his cock fitting so perfectly inside me. The friction against my walls pushed me toward the edge.

I jerked against him, rocking forward and back so hard it almost hurt, but the pleasure derived from each clash of our bodies far outweighed it. The events of the day—the worries and doubts and demands that hit us from all angles drifted away with each pump, replaced by nothing but *need*.

He grew harder, tightening in the already snug pace, and I locked eyes with him. The shock wasn't hidden in his molten blues, and it made me fly apart.

Rory's hand covered my own mouth as I moaned, unable to contain the explosion of ecstasy inside me. I came long after he'd finished but he kept slowly lifting my hips and bringing me back down, drawing out my orgasm until I was dizzy.

My thighs quivered as I came down, breathing deeply to reorient myself. He licked the tips of my fingers as I withdrew my hand from his mouth and slid off of him and back to my seat.

He shook his head as he zipped up and I smirked at him. I couldn't help but notice the closer I grew to Rory, the more I got dangerously close to succeeding as a very *bad girl*.

"Here we are, Mr. Jackson." Dave's voice startled us out of our silent stare down, and heat rushed all over my skin.

A loophole threesome had been accomplished and while I tried to convince myself the driver was oblivious; I knew there was no way.

"Thanks, Dave," Rory said, sliding out of the car behind me.

My legs shook as I walked toward my front door, my muscles still quivering from the orgasm Rory had perfectly orchestrated.

"What's number eight?" Rory asked as he shut the door behind us.

"Hmm?" I asked, my head buzzing with pleasure.

He chuckled, pushing my wild hair back from my face. "You said we'd check off number eight, too. What was it?"

"Oh," I said, laughing. "Have sex in a car."

Wrapping his arms around me, he molded my already pliant body against every hard plane of his. "Can't wait to finish the list."

"In a hurry to get it over with?" I teased.

He nipped at my bottom lip. "We'll make one together once I satisfy yours."

"Mmm," I moaned, planting my lips against his. "You are really good at *satisfying* me."

"Careful, Red. Keep talking like that, and I'll spout off another number."

I went slack in his arms, and he caught me easily. "I want you in my bed, but more in a *NetflixandChill* sort of way." I squinted at him. "Is that okay? At least for an hour?" I needed time to recharge. Sex with Rory—no matter how long or how quick—spent every ounce of my energy to the point of turning me into a puddle.

He nuzzled my neck with his nose before sweeping an arm behind my knees. He cradled me to his massive chest and walked toward my bedroom. "We've got all the time in the world, Red."

The truth behind his words caught up in my heart, sending it flying as high as it had when he'd said he loved me. The three-month term didn't matter anymore. Rory was mine.

CHAPTER 15

RORY

"YOU AREN'T WEARING A TIE," Paige said as she stepped onto her front porch, her black pumps clicking against the concrete.

Damn those shoes. There were too many good memories attached to them—like the spike digging into my back as I buried myself between her thighs—and she *knew* it. The woman was wicked and had worn them to torture me.

"Ties are usually only good for one thing, and I doubt there will be a bedpost for me to secure your wrists to at this event." I smoothed my hands down the all black tux I wore. "Is it mandatory?" I asked after relishing the flush of her cheeks.

She blinked rapidly before focusing on me. "What? I'm sorry, I was just *picturing* it."

I stepped up to her, wrapping one hand around her waist. Her lips were painted a perfect red that I didn't dare smear; instead I hovered my mouth just above hers. "That can go on *our* list."

Her breath hitched enough to make her pert breasts graze against my chest. "Maybe we can make an amendment to mine after the event? If you can manage to track down a tie, that is." She laughed as she closed my mouth that had dropped open.

I released my hold on her. "Oh, I'll tear it off someone's neck if it means you'll let me strip you bare, tie you up, and use my tongue to make you come until you can't take it a second more. Can you *picture* it? Your body quaking from release after release, limp and sated while you relinquish every ounce of control?"

She gasped but the heat in her eyes told me exactly what I already knew—my redhead was up for anything, as long as it was with me. The notion made my chest puff out a little more than usual. Hell, it had almost been in a permanent prideful position since we'd exchanged *I love you's* two weeks ago. Something I never expected would happen to me, let alone me be the first one to say it.

"We don't have to go," I said, watching the heat fill her eyes the longer I held her to me.

She pushed against my chest, putting enough distance between us to catch the cool breeze of the night air. "We do. Laying low worked, cooling off the heat the press kept putting on us, but now it's time to remind them of the relationship we have..."

"And you have something to prove," I finished for her.

"I do not."

"You're a terrible liar." I grinned at her, resolved to take her hand instead of her body.

"Fine," she said, allowing me to lead her to the car. "If it means maintaining my forward progression in the company and ensuring my funding for the shelter project, then yes, I want to show the world that I'm yours and it's not the end of the fucking world."

I stopped our movements, my eyes widening at her

quick mood shift. It wasn't the first time she jumped tracks on me in the last couple weeks, and I wondered if she wasn't being entirely honest about the pressure hitting her at work. I grinned at her, grabbing a handful of her perfect ass. "God I love it when you say that."

"Fucking?" She asked, a laugh on her lips.

I trailed one finger down the line of her jaw. "You're mine." Her body shifted closer to me, almost as if a magnet tugged on her core. I called on all the willpower I possessed and kissed the back of her hand. "We leave. Now."

She sucked her teeth, snapping out of it. "Right."

Twenty minutes later she wove her arm through mine as we entered Mark Chase's *Night For Wounded Warriors* event. The rooftop setting marveled that of the Four Season's gala I'd attended on Paige's behalf—the memory of that night made me hard just thinking about it. I focused on the view, assuring my dick he'd have his moment with her later. The sun had just set, leaving the sky an inky-blue with hints of stars piercing it. Twinkle lights offered an intimate setting despite the incredibly large space, and waiters casually made their way through the groups of people dressed in their best black-tie attire.

Grabbing a couple of champagne flutes, I offered one to Paige. She smirked but didn't bring the drink to her lips.

"What's so amusing?" I asked, wincing from the sugary sweetness the champagne left in my mouth. I was always going to be a beer or scotch kind of guy. Something flashed behind her eyes, but she quickly blinked it away before I could register what it had been, if anything at all.

"I was just thinking I've only seen one view better than this." She motioned toward the skyline, and it took me a minute before the memory hit me. The night I'd brought her to my place and fucked her on my balcony.

"Is that all you ever think about?" I asked, pretending to be offended. The fact that she wanted me as badly and as often as I wanted her—despite making love almost every day this week—only made me love her that much more.

She smacked my chest before taking the flute out of my hands. "I'll hunt you down something stronger."

"It's fine," I said quickly. I hadn't had a hard drink in public since the night I'd been arrested for the brawl. The same night of the gala at the Four Seasons. I'd been on my best behavior, and I knew too much liquor only made my already short fuse shorter. Plus, we'd just sailed through playoffs and were on our way to the Stanley Cup. Staying sober seemed responsible. Boring, but responsible.

Paige reached up and smoothed a crease between my brow. "Relax. I'm here." She squeezed my hand. "And you've killed yourself in the rink all week. You deserve a drink." She winked, but I didn't let go of her hand, instead electing to follow her to the bar. Paige was like a lifeline—as long as we stayed connected nothing could touch us, paparazzi or vengeful puck bunnies alike.

The bar had been stationed before one of the exposed corners of the rooftop—the massive wooden structure decorated with a back-lit ice sculpture depicting the raising of the flag on Iwo Jima. Chase had been a well-known advocate for Wounded Warriors, and it was no surprise he'd sprung for the best at this event—which was one of thirty taking place in various portions of the country throughout the year, or so Paige had told me.

I'd always liked this organization and made an effort to contribute annually, but this event mattered more to Paige's father who'd supported the troops and veterans—and made sure their company did as well. I knew it was the main reason she'd asked me to come and maybe that was the explanation behind her quick shifts in mood lately. The pressure to please her father was bigger than ever now that she was publically dating...*me*. Balancing who she was supposed to be with who she wanted to be—who she really was—was taking a toll.

"Two fingers of scotch," Paige asked the tender. "And a water, please."

I squeezed her hand. "We have a driver tonight," I whispered in her ear. "You can indulge too."

She laughed, but the sound was tense. "I didn't drink enough water today. I'll have one later."

I took my offered drink from the tender and slipped a twenty into the crystal vase used for collecting tips. Paige reclaimed my arm, and we weaved through the crowd, stopping each time she needed to mingle with someone. I drank my scotch plus one more and enjoyed watching her work the crowd. The woman never missed an opportunity to make new business acquaintances, and the sharpness of her mind turned me on almost as much as her tenacity for getting me into bed.

"Rory Jackson," A slightly familiar voice took my attention off of Paige who spoke to a few people across the rooftop. I turned slightly, finding an Ontario enforcer—one of our biggest rivals and the same team that asshole Adkins played for. I glanced around the area, scanning for his face. It didn't matter that Gage and Helen had worked their shit out, I still hated Adkins on principal, and he was the last person I wanted to see tonight. Trevor was a close second.

"Trevor," I said, finishing the scotch in my glass. "Adkins with you tonight?" The muscles in my shoulders tensed as I waited for him to answer.

"No, he and the trophy wife are off buying diamonds or some shit."

A fraction of the tension coiling my muscles relaxed.

"Rory?" Paige's voice came at me as she returned to her spot by my side. She took my empty glass and handed me a fresh one. I instantly took a large gulp.

The silence between the three of us bordered on awkward as I waited for Trevor to leave now that he'd made his presence known. "Thanks," I finally said to Paige, who stood rigid next to me as her eyes jumped between Trevor and me.

"Red is a new color for you, Jackson." He pointed to Paige with the long-neck in his hand. "Thought you liked the blonde bunnies."

Instinctively my fist clenched tightly around the glass in my hand, his slow gaze lingering a little too long on Paige. I opened my mouth, but Paige's response cut me off.

"Oh," she said. "You're Trevor Hewitt. Ontario's enforcer. Sorry about your loss last week. Must've been rough."

I smirked and fell a little more in love with her if that was possible.

Trevor had the gall to look impressed. "She's smart too? Now that is really off the mark for you, Jackson."

I shifted my weight, his tone making my skin itch. "We're not all prone to the senseless, Hewitt."

"Since when?" He took another swig of his beer, his lazy gaze falling on Paige again. "Don't let him fool you, sweetheart. Not three months ago he was plowing through a haystack of traveling bunnies and tossing them like used cups."

"Still sore about that beatdown I gave you then?" Every muscle I had flexed. "A little petty to goad me at a charity event. Save it for the game. I'll remind you how my fist feels then." I made my tone as sharp as a razor, my chest tightening from the ache in my bones to knock the greedy look off his face as he kept ogling Paige.

She tugged on my arm. "Come with me, will you? I'm dying to show you this ice sculpture," she said, clearly giving me a free out from the heated situation. We'd already seen the sculpture, but I turned to follow her. We stopped at a clear space near the bar, and she reached up to cup my face.

"Rory, look at me," she said, and I locked onto her emerald green eyes. "Remember why we're here?"

I nodded, breathing deep but not enough to squash the adrenaline in my blood.

"And you remember what I want to do afterward?" she smirked at me. "We can't do that unless you're a good boy."

A smile finally cracked my tight lips, and I sighed, trailing a finger down her cheek. "You're wicked, Red. Smart, but wicked."

"Just as you like it," she whispered, slipping her hand beneath my tux jacket and rubbing her palm across my abs. I closed my eyes, leaning my forehead against hers as I often did to calm my raging nerves. Something about Paige always kept me grounded whenever I felt like I was going off the rails.

After a moment she jolted underneath me, turning around as if someone had tapped her on the shoulder. "Yes?" She asked, a hint of annoyance in her tone.

"I forgot to give you something, sweetheart." Trevor's gaze didn't leave mine as he handed Paige a business card with a hand written number on it. "For when he's licked your flavor clean. Never seen a bunny hold his interest beyond a night. You must be...*talented*." He cut his eyes to Paige for a moment before bringing them back to me. "The second you realize Jackson is useless know that I'd love to discover just how talented you are."

The energy shifted in the atmosphere around me. He'd hit upon two of my biggest triggers—calling me useless and hitting on Paige.

One second I'd swam in the calm waters that Paige's presence surrounded me in. The next I was a maelstrom seeing red. I launched at Hewitt as if we were on the ice, and sent him crashing straight through the sculpture we'd been pretending to look at moments ago. It shattered in huge chunks both behind and in front of the bar.

I dove on top of Hewitt, laying into him with a right hook he should have memorized from our past games—but this wasn't to prevent a goal, this was to prove a point. No one spoke to Paige like that. Ever. Hewitt managed a crack at my jaw, but I recovered quicker than he could blink, landing another blow hard enough to make him limp. I pulled my fist back, readying for another punch to be sure he got the message.

"Rory Jackson!" The sharp tone of Paige's voice was the only thing capable of jerking me out of myself. I snapped out of it, slowly returning to reality, one where I hadn't even registered the group of younger guys surrounding us with their phones out and cameras rolling. *Fuck, this would hit the media in minutes.*

I pushed off the floor, craning my neck until I found her —along with the entire party—staring at me. The hurt in her eyes crushed the center of my chest harder than any physical blow could. She looked at me like I'd betrayed her and the sight made me want to drop to my fucking knees before her.

"Paige—"

She held her hand up to stop me, smoothing the lines of her dress as security rushed passed her. They hefted Hewitt off the floor.

"Just a misunderstanding, gentlemen." Hewitt swiped at some blood on the corner of his mouth. "No need to cause more of a scene. I'll cover the damages." He glanced at the crowd. "Sorry about that, folks. Little anxious to get back in the rink with this one, seeing as we'll be going against each other for the Stanley Cup in a couple weeks." He gestured to me, but I only spared him a glance before I returned focus to Paige. While he was cleaning up my mess —saying all the things I should've—I was watching the light go out behind Paige's eyes.

She finally broke our locked eyes, shaking her head as she walked inside the building, holding her grace, her composure, because apparently I fucking couldn't. For a second I hesitated, my muscles locked from adrenaline. Then I *ran*, chased after her faster than when I was on the ice. I grabbed her arm outside the elevator bank, spinning her to face me.

"Paige—"

"Don't." She cut me off again. Tears were in her eyes, and she held her stomach as she took a deep breath.

I'd made her sick.

She opened her mouth to speak but jolted again, and I did too as my cell buzzed in my pocket. Where she reached for hers, I stood absolutely still, silently begging her to forgive me.

She clenched her eyes shut after reading the message on her screen, the motion forcing the tears to roll down her cheeks. "I could've handled Trevor on my own," she said. "I didn't need the macho crap."

"I know," I said. "I can't control it. Sometimes—"

"I know. Trust me." She stepped toward me, placing a small kiss on my lips. "I fell in love you with you, Rory. Every part of you." More tears as she slipped her phone back into her small purse. "But you just cost me everything."

She could've hit me in the gut with a sledgehammer, and I would've been in less pain than I was in that instant. The tightrope across my chest cinched, threatening to crack my bones. I didn't need to see the screen to know what was on it. Her father's vow...my actions...she'd just lost her company.

I parted my lips, searching for the right words. Words that would win me her heart—her trust—back. Another bucket of ice water crashed over my head, turning my blood cold.

She'd needed me to be man enough to restrain myself unless the situation desperately called for it and tonight's did it. How many other nights would there be where I did this to her?

Fuck.

A sharp twinge wracked my insides like I'd drank nothing but pure acid all night.

Paige deserved better than this. Better than me. She always had. And I was the dumbass for thinking I was strong enough to give it to her.

"Rory..." she said my name with a tear stained voice. "Let's go—"

"No." I was the one to cut her off this time. I clenched my eyes shut, giving myself a moment to find the mask I needed to do right by her. After a few seconds, I opened my eyes and looked at her like she was any bunny from my past I wanted to get rid of. "You go. I don't need this hassle."

She flinched as if I'd slapped her, her hand once again flying to her stomach.

Good. She should be disgusted with me.

"What?" Anger flashed behind her wet eyes.

I shrugged, the motion more painful than knowing I would never touch her again. "This was fun and all, but I'm done being your go-to bad-boy for a fucking list."

"You don't mean that," she said, sucking in a stuttered breath.

I turned my back on her, unable to hold the casual mask with her eyes on me. My resolve shook when she reached out and touched my shoulder. I was seconds away from breaking, from dropping the act and being the selfish asshole who stayed with her just to ruin her some more.

"I've lost everything tonight, already," she whispered. "Don't make me lose you, too."

She'd lost her dream, her company, because of *me*. I'd known the terms her father had placed upon her once she'd started a relationship with me—I'd known them and still fucking slipped. I jerked out from underneath her touch, glancing over my shoulder with eyes I hoped were as cold as ice. She took a few steps away from me like she'd just happened upon a stranger...a dangerous stranger.

"Can't lose what you never had, Red."

A tiny gasp and one more tear. One more slice to the heart I never knew I had.

Then she straightened her spine, shifting from wounded bird to fearsome lioness in an instant. She gave me one nod and backed into the elevator, never losing my eyes until the doors slid closed, taking the only woman I ever loved away from me for good.

CHAPTER 16

PAIGE

"PAIGE, won't you reconsider merely taking a small leave of absence?" My father paced in front of my desk as I packed some of the more important items away in the box I had on top of it. "I was too harsh last night. I should've waited to speak to you in person."

I cut my eyes to him, battling the anger I had inside. I couldn't decide which was worse, that I understood his actions from a business standpoint, or that I felt beyond betrayed as his daughter? I couldn't have it both ways, but even as I stood there, contemplating how best to professionally handle the situation, I knew where my heart lied.

"You handed me an impossible ultimatum—having to choose between the company I love, the dreams I have for the future, and the *man* I love." His eyebrows rose at my use of the L-word. "And to make matters worse, you didn't even give me the chance to explain last night. You simply texted and said I was fired. A text!" I shook my head. "Do you realize how many more instances like this will happen to me in my future?" Even one without Rory in it. The thought had my heart shattering all over again, but I kept my face even. "Regardless of who is by my side, or if I'm alone forever, there will always be someone in the media out to get me. Just as they have been you for years."

I took a deep breath, forcing the emotions flooding my body to calm.

"You threatened me over fear of a public relations fiasco and some consumer backlash bullshit. *You* pushed me to this exit." I scooped the box off the desk and walked around it, stopping just in front of him. "I hope to God you pulled the reports I told you to. Hope you realize how much this company's increase in profit margins, employment retainability, and product innovation rose after I implemented more movements than you know what to do with."

I walked to the doors of what had been my second home since childhood. A heavy, sick weight set on my chest but I swallowed past it.

"Paige?"

The softness in my father's voice forced me to turn and look at him.

"Was it worth it?" His eyes fell to my belly, and I shifted the box in my hands, suddenly worried he could see right through me.

Thoughts of Rory flooded my mind—as did the two pink lines on the test I'd taken right before he'd picked me up last night for the event. I was going to tell him after the party. After I'd had time to get my head on straight. Then all hell had broken loose because he couldn't keep hold of his temper. And even after all that—after knowing I'd lost my dream shelter and my position in this company because of the terms my father had set around my relationship with Rory— I'd forgiven him before he'd even reached me at the elevators.

His cold, hurtful tone, his emotionless eyes as he brushed our relationship off as nothing more than the contract it had started off as had shattered my heart into a thousand tiny pieces. He'd called me a hassle and the realization that *I* was the one thing he wasn't willing to fight for had left me a sopping, broken mess.

Or that could be the hormones. Maybe a combo of both.

Either way, I'd managed to pull myself together long enough to come into the office today and give my father a piece of my mind. While his temper had cooled overnight, mine had not, and I was done being treated like a little girl playing at running a corporation.

I held my head high, finally prepared to answer my father. "Ask yourself that question when the company feels the sting of my absence. I was your biggest asset. Now I'm your biggest competition." I let the doors swing shut as I walked through them, and refused to look back.

"When do you start at *Wilson & Rowe's*?" Bailey asked as she sat next to me at *Nine's* bar.

Jeannine slid an ice water toward me, eyeing it like it was poison. "Are you sure this doesn't call for scotch? Seems like the type of situation in which there is scotch."

"Stop it, Jeannine," Bailey chided, placing her hand on my back. "She needs a clear head."

"She needs to get drunk," Jeannine challenged, and the two took up a staring competition of epic proportions.

The restaurant had been closed for a couple of hours and enough time had passed for me to work up just enough courage to say what I needed to.

"Trust me. I need water." I swallowed the nerves jolting inside me. "I'm pregnant."

Jeannine dropped the bottle of scotch she'd pulled off the shelf, the glass thunking against the thankfully padded flooring.

"And to answer your first question," I continued, eyeing Bailey. "It's an open invitation to come work whenever I want. I haven't given them a final answer yet because..." I gestured to my still flat stomach, completely at a loss...not about *Wilson & Rowe's* of course, but about everything else.

I'd been raised to top the company time and time again, and now they'd offered to let me head up their corporate offices here in Seattle. The business side of it was smart— they offered me more money than I made in my previous VP position, and they ensured me the freedom to take the line in a new direction if that was my vision. They'd wanted me bad after we'd crushed them in sales this fiscal year, and I knew I could make a real difference there. It was the personal side, the roots I had in my family's company, which made me feel dirtier than any list ever could.

Bailey let out a squeal, her eyes already brimming with tears. Jeannine scooped the bottle off the floor, twisted off the cap and took a shot.

"Oh my God, Paige," Bailey said, wrapping her arms around me, her own protruding belly grazing my knee as she leaned over me. "Wait," she pulled back, her face going from overjoyed to serious in a blink. "Are you happy? Devastated? You can tell us. It's okay. Just because I'm pregnant doesn't mean you have to be happy about it." The nervous ramble was comforting in ways I didn't even realize. *Thank God for my girls.*

"Are you in there?" Jeannine asked, poking my shoulder after I remained silent for too long.

"I think so," I said, patting the center of my chest that hadn't stopped aching since last night.

"Have you told him?" Jeannine asked, setting the bottle on the bar.

"I was going to but then last night happened."

"What were you going to say?" Bailey asked, resting her hand on my knee.

I shrugged. The first time I noticed I was late I had panicked. I was on birth control, and there was no reason for me to believe it wasn't performing properly—but there was that *one* day I'd taken a pill a few hours late. Honestly, when I'd done it, I hadn't thought I'd be having sex that night, but it was the same night Rory had first taken me to his loft.

A few hours changed everything.

"You're killing me with the silence, Paige." Bailey's eyes were growing more frantic by the second. "What was your initial reaction when you saw the test?"

The mom in her couldn't help but analyze me, and I loved her for it. A smile tugged at my lips as the memory of the two pink lines as they came into view. "Panic. Terror. But also..." I touched my belly, attempting to feel what I knew I couldn't possibly feel so soon. "Elation. Hope. I pictured a blue eyed blond boy tearing up my house. I imagined Rory reading to him at bedtime. I saw him sitting on my knee at games like Lettie does with you." I eyed Bailey, swiping at the tears that pooled in the corner of my eyes. "Being a mom isn't...*wasn't* part of my plan. But neither was Rory. And even though we're done, I can't imagine not having this piece of him."

I looked back and forth between the two girls, begging for guidance.

"Fuck," Jeannine said, chugging down her own glass of

water. "See what happens when you start checking things off a dirty-girl list? You should never have made it." She chuckled, and the joke broke the tension in my chest.

I laughed and cried and then cried some more.

"What are you going to do with the time off?" Jeannine asked after we'd reeled it in, mostly. She'd stripped off her chef's jacket and donned the black tank top she wore underneath it. "Finish the list?" She joked again.

"Seriously?" Bailey chided.

"Why not? It got her this far?" She chuckled, and I burst out laughing.

"God you're evil." Bailey shook her head, but a smile lit up her eyes as she looked at me. "You could call him," she said. "Use your family's jet and whisk him away to the Bahamas."

"Because that makes sense."

"I'd do it if I had the time and a man who could keep up with me." Jeannine leaned her elbows on the bar. "Girl has got a point. Think about it. Nothing but sun and sand and a half naked *number seven* for a couple of weeks. Plus, you're not showing yet so you can still pull off a bikini."

"I can't. He ended it—"

"Oh bullshit," Jeannine cut me off. "The guy is pushing you away. Anyone can see that."

I sighed. "And that isn't code for *I love you*. You weren't there. You didn't see the way he looked at me. Like I was nothing but a fun challenge he couldn't say no to." The truth of the statement stung my chest all over again.

She threw her hands up. "You're impossible. You *love* him. He loves you. This can't be that difficult."

"It's true. He was at the house last night, mopey as hell and whining like a puppy," Bailey said. "I just didn't know why. But now that I do...well, it all makes sense. He loves you, Paige, no matter what he said."

"See! Get him!" Jeannine shouted.

I arched an eyebrow at her. I wanted to say that he'd never loved me, that it had been an act all along, but I couldn't bring myself to believe it. It had felt too real to be a lie. Perhaps I was lying to myself.

Bailey rolled her eyes. "We can't all wear the professional-reckless-goddess crown that you do, Nine."

She snapped her fingers, pointing at me. "She was so close to stealing it too! How many left do you have on the list? Two?"

"Three." I scooted my empty water glass to her, and she poured a fresh wave for me. "Rory helped me cross off more than just his number."

"I assumed. After the bathroom incident." She motioned toward the restaurant's restrooms, and I blushed. The memory was fresh and real and I could practically feel the man between my thighs. Even after he'd crushed my heart, I still ached for his touch. *God, I need to get a grip.*

"What bathroom incident?" Bailey squeaked beside me. "What'd I miss?"

"Nothing," I said. Nothing I needed to think about ever again. The sooner I accepted the reality that Rory didn't think I was worth fighting for the sooner I could sort through the more important things on my mind—like carrying his child while he didn't have a clue.

Fuck my life.

"I vote finish it," Jeannine continued, still on the damn list topic. "If you're not going to explore the endless possibilities with number seven, at least finish what you started."

"Good Lord, you won't let it drop until I do, will you?" I

snorted. "You think a major heartbreak and surprise pregnancy would be enough to let a girl off the hook."

She grinned and shook her head. "Nope. This is why I'm here. I've always been the one to push you when you needed it. Now you've found a man who can do even better than me, and you're letting him go?" She tsked me. "The dirty-girl goddess frowns on your lack of follow through."

"He dumped me!" I shouted, but she didn't accept it. "Fine." I smacked my glass down and raised up on my barstool to lean over the bar, grabbing Jeannine around her neck. Before she could blink I planted my lips on hers, crushing them with all the frustration I had pulsing inside me. She wanted me to get my list done? This was number four.

She didn't freeze—not like I expected, but instead moved her lips against mine. It wasn't awful, just awkward as hell. I'd loved this woman for half my life and yet, there was no spark of need as we kissed. *Well, that settled that then.*

I sank back down on the barstool, returning to sipping my water as I ignored the wide-eyed, gaping stare from Bailey. Finally, she closed her mouth and tilted her head. "Why'd you pick her?"

Another laugh ripped from my throat.

"Obviously she has a thing for blonds. Look at Rory," Jeannine said, waving Bailey away.

Bailey chuckled. "I *so* didn't need to be witness to that."

"Another one off the list. Now you have to give me a break," I said, eyeing Jeannine.

She smiled at me, genuine concern in her eyes. I know she only pressed the subject to make me laugh, to distract me from the royally *fuckedupness* my life had spiraled into overnight—and I loved her for it. Loved Bailey for comforting me in the only way someone who totally understood could—she hadn't exactly planned for her bun in the oven either.

I sighed, thankful for the two women in my life who made the hardest day of mine seem a little less dark.

Now, if only they could stitch my heart back together, we'd be in business.

CHAPTER 17

RORY

CRASH! I slammed Bentley into the boards, harder than necessary for a practice.

"Fuck," Bentley groaned as he pushed himself up off the ice. "Man, I've kept my mouth shut for weeks."

"Ontario won't go easy on you. I won't either." I skated off, trying and failing to keep Trevor Hewitt, and the night he ruined my life out of my head.

It had been a week since I'd forced Paige to see me as the asshole everyone else did. A week since I'd been in love and happy for the first time in my life before I fucked it all up, just as I knew I would. It hurt like fucking hell, but I knew she was a million times better off without me in her life. She'd move on, marry a Kennedy, and have the perfect life she'd been groomed for. She'd be happy. Well...content, at least.

That's not your Red, and you know it.

She's not mine anymore. Shut the fuck up.

This battle with myself hadn't let up for even a second since that night. And today I was letting that frustration out on the ice.

"Rory," Coach called me to the box after I'd checked another teammate into the boards as hard as possible.

I skidded to a stop before him, slipping inside and sinking down on the bench next to him.

"You all right?" he asked.

"Fine."

"Ready to play on Saturday?"

"Absolutely." Game one of the Stanley Cup Finals. My dream. And I was more than ready. After all, if I couldn't have the dream of Paige, I'd sure as fuck nail this one.

"You seem to be working out something out there. Want to let me in?" He crossed his arms over his chest.

"Nope." I took a swig of water from one of the many bottles in the box.

"Fine. You're looking great. Whatever it is you're doing, keep doing it." He clapped me on the back. "But not today. Go shower up."

I bolted off the bench. "But Coach!" There was still an hour left in practice and I'd only just warmed up.

He shook his head. "I said you're doing great. Just save it for Ontario. I don't need my players hurt because something lit a fire under you. Rest up."

I huffed, knowing he had a point. "Yes, sir."

I unlaced my skates and stalked toward the locker room. Even as I showered, I itched to unleash more pain on anyone who could take it. Coach had said something had lit a fire under me, but it wasn't *something*. It was *someone*. My Red. The woman had made my soul blaze from the second I'd touched her. She was all consuming, and for the briefest of moments, I breathed fire. Now, with the absence of her, all that made me up was rage. I stood under the water until my skin puckered and my blood ran slightly cooler.

"Bro," Gage nodded to me as I toweled off. He and the

rest of the team had just funneled in from practice. "You good?"

I flipped him off.

"Okay, wrong question." Gage started stripping off his gear at his locker next to mine. He shook his head, his knowing eyes too judgy for my liking. "You know—"

"Don't, man. Don't say a fucking word."

Gage stood, his height just barely beating mine. "Fuck you. You're being an idiot."

"Hey now, kids," Warren chided from behind Gage. "We're all bros here remember?"

"Shut up!" Both Gage and I snapped in unison. Warren flipped us both off and headed to the showers.

"You can't keep doing this to yourself." Gage continued.

"I'm not doing anything."

"Bullshit. Paige is a wreck. You're being a bigger asshole than usual..."

Her name on his lips snapped my attention up to him, breaking my rage-wall. "She's a wreck?"

What did you think she'd be asshole? You think a week goes by and she's skipping down easy street?

"Yeah," Gage crossed his arms over his chest. "Not that I'm supposed to tell you that." He raked his hands through his hair.

"What else did Bailey say?" I asked, suddenly desperate to be in the know. How could I simultaneously want to soothe Paige's pain *and* be the cause of it?

Because it will be better for her in the long run. You ruin everything. Right.

Something flashed behind Gage's eyes, but he quickly started digging through his locker. "I don't know, man. Stuff. Why did you do it?"

I shrugged. "It wasn't real. It was a challenge, and I failed."

"Bullshit."

I punched my locker closed, knowing I couldn't lie to my best friend. "She deserves better. It was the only way I knew how to ensure she'd get what she deserved one day."

"She deserved you." Gage forced me to look him in the eye. "You loved her. Still do. Why are you making it so difficult?"

"Because! There won't be a time in my life that I'm good enough for her!"

"And there hasn't been one time in mine that I've been good enough for Bailey, but we fucking make it work. That's what love is! She makes you better, and you take care of her."

I rested my head against my closed locker, the cool metal searing my heated skin. "Paige. Deserves. Better. I cost her everything, and I'll never be in a position to hurt her again."

"Fine, man. You want to ruin your life and hers. Fine. I can't stop you." He slammed his locker shut. "Just know you're making the biggest mistake of your life." He stomped toward the showers, leaving me shaking with adrenaline.

I knew he was right. I knew Paige was it for me. No one would ever be close to what she meant to me. That's why I did what I did. Because I loved her and wanted her to have the life she'd always dreamed of. The one where she ran her family company and built her dream shelters all over the country. One with someone who treated her like the queen she was.

And I only hoped that without me in the picture, her father had changed his mind on his ultimatum.

"Jackson," Bentley called my name from the exit.

"What?" I snapped, jerking my head up toward him.

He walked to me, his hands raised. "Fucking chill, man. That redhead is outside asking for you."

My heart jolted in my chest, the little bitch having the dare to hope. "Fucking tell her I'm not here."

"Fuck you. I'm not your messenger."

I arched my head to the ceiling. *Why are you here, Paige?* Why couldn't she stay away?

The same reason you've practically been handcuffing yourself to your bed every night to keep from going to her.

Had my cold goodbye on the rooftop not been convincing enough? What else did I have to do to get her to believe I was the asshole everyone said I was?

I slipped a shirt over my head, unable to take the battle a second longer, and stepped into the hallway. There she was, as gorgeous as ever, hell, even more so since it had been a week since I saw her last. I had stayed away from the press, too, so I hadn't even seen a picture of her. I hadn't wanted to; it was too painful. And seeing her in person, now? Fuck, might as well rip my heart out and put it in a blender.

Her green eyes widened as she took me in and I self-consciously rubbed at the scruff decorating my chin. She was lucky I'd showered at all today. Shaving, eating, sleeping—they'd all fallen off my radar the second I'd forced her from my life.

"Hi," she said, her voice smaller than I'd ever heard it.

"What are you doing here?" I snapped, the anger from my conversation with Gage offering the perfect asshole tone I needed to use with her.

Her perfect red lips popped into the shape of an O before she straightened her spine. "I need to discuss something with you."

I shook my head. "No, you don't." God, I wanted to

keep her talking. Just to hear her voice. *You want more than that.*

"Yes. It's important."

"Another contract?" I pulled out my best smirk. "I'm all booked now." *I love you. I need you. I'm sorry.*

She sighed. "Stop. Please? I can tell this isn't you."

"You don't know me." I swallowed hard, praying she couldn't see the Grecian battle raging inside me, fighting off every instinct that screamed out to touch her. Hold her. Beg for her to take me back.

"That's a lie. I know you better than anyone ever has."

"Whatever. Look, I've got to go." I turned back toward the locker room, the move searing every inch of my insides.

"Rory," she said, reaching out and touching my arm to stop me. Her fingers singed the bare skin, and I clenched my jaw to stop myself from grabbing her and kissing the breath out of her. She took the flex offensively, jerking her hand back as if I were going to bite. "I really need to talk to you."

Everything in me wanted to know what she had to say, wanted to listen to her read a fucking menu if meant she kept talking, but the one part of me that truly loved her knew I couldn't. "I'm already late," I said. "Hot date tonight, so, whatever is why don't you email it? Or just forget about it." I spared her one last glance, just quick enough to catch the angry tears in her eyes before I shut the door in her face.

"What was that about?" Gage asked as he toweled his hair.

"I'm an asshole." I snapped.

"Fuck, man what *was* that?" His eyes darted to the door and back to me. "Was it Paige?"

"Why does it matter?"

"What did she say?" The urgency in his tone had all my nerves on edge.

"Gage?"

"What did she say?" He practically growled.

"Nothing, man!" I shook my head. "I didn't let her. I told her off. It's better for her!" I didn't want to have this fucking argument again.

Gage threw his massive arms in the air, searching the area for something to throw. With only the bench in reach, he took a steadying breath. Dude was way more in control than I was. "Fuck my life!" He screamed.

"What is up your ass, man?"

"Bailey is going to *fucking* kill me, that's what."

A knot formed in my stomach. "What are you talking about?"

"What I'm not *supposed* to be talking about." He pinched the bridge of his nose before looking up at me. "I need you to be honest with me, man. Do you love her?"

I slit my eyes at him. "You know I do. That's why I have to make her leave me—"

"Fuck your twisted way of protecting her. Of giving her a better life. Do you *love* her? Like, do anything for her kind of love?"

"You think I'd kill myself like this over someone who I didn't?" I shrugged. "I'm in hell without her, but I'm willing to take that shit if it means she gets what she wants out of life. Things I can't possibly give her."

"All right. This conversation never happened." Gage sighed. "She left her father's company."

"What?"

"Yeah. Basically told him to fuck himself for trying to make her choose between work and you."

I'm such an asshole.

"But her shelter. The funding..."

"Didn't matter. She still left."

I raked my fingers through my hair. "Fuck."

"There's more, but you should really let her tell you."

I cut my eyes to him. "How? How can there be *more* than that?"

He paced the length of the bench before us, battling with himself. "Fucking hell, man Bailey is going to chop something off of me..."

"I don't care, bro! You're fucking scaring me!"

"It's not really my place—"

"Gage." My tone had the death threat warning that stopped his pacing.

"Paige is..." he swallowed hard like the words were spikes coming out of his mouth. "Pregnant."

I fell down, my ass hitting the bench with a loud smack. The edges of my vision went blurry—shiny like a sparkling fog had suddenly filled the locker room. *Pregnant*. The word repeated itself in my head and my heart raced. The image of a green-eyed, redheaded princess popped behind my fog covered eyes—she'd have a laugh like her mother's. And a temper like mine.

"Rory?" Gage's hand was on my shoulder, but his voice sounded far away.

The vision turned. One where Paige was left to raise our daughter alone all because I'd thought she'd be better off without me. No fucking way. She was *mine*. And if took an eternity I'd spend every day making up for all the shit I'd fucked up.

"Fuck, she thinks I don't care about her!" I stood up, my eyes clearing. "She thinks I used her."

"Wasn't that your goal?" Gage said, looking at me with a smug face.

"I really am an asshole."

He nodded. "There is time to make this right."

"Right," I said the word, withdrawing into myself. How could I possibly prove it to her? Prove to her I loved her more than anything on this entire fucking planet? A light clicked on in my overcrowded brain, and I snapped my eyes to Gage. "I know what I have to do."

I just hoped it would be enough.

CHAPTER 18

PAIGE

"ARE you sure you don't want to talk to—" Kelsey stopped speaking as I eyed her from the office in my home. She'd come with me when I'd left CranBaby with the intention of working for me at Wilson and Rowe. I had yet to accept their offer, though. I was currently content to wrap up some projects from home as I figured out the best course of action for us next.

I smoothed my hand over my tummy, as I did every time I thought the word *us* instead of *me*. My life had changed in the course of a few weeks, but I wouldn't take a second of it back.

Maybe Rory. I might take him back.

I shoved the thought away, remembering how he wouldn't even make time for me when I'd come to his practice, ready to tell him about the baby. I wasn't going to ask him for anything. I just thought he had the right to know. Whether he cared or not, that would be up to him.

You know he would care.

I forced the voice in my head to shut up. She was such a traitor, always pulling up memories that proved he loved me. How could she believe that when all recent evidence pointed to the contrary. He'd said he was fucking dating! He moved on quicker than I could blink.

"I apologize," I said, realizing Kelsey was still standing there. "What were you saying?"

"He called again."

I sighed. Rory had tried to call every day for the past week. I'd ignored him. And the flowers. And the attempt when he knocked on my door earlier in the week. I'd given him an olive branch at the practice that day, and he'd thrown it in the garbage...just like me. I couldn't continue to play his game and let him hurt me all over again. Especially now that I was responsible for more than one heart.

"That's unfortunate." I pulled up my email on my Mac, prepared to write to the contractors about my inability to continue funding the project of my dreams. I'd pooled all the resources and assets I had, and it hadn't been enough to see the project to completion, even with my considerable savings. I'd been avoiding writing this email all week. "Please continue to ignore the calls. And make me aware if he shows up on the property again, all right?"

She looked down at me with worry in her eyes. "Maybe he's sorry."

"Maybe he is. Maybe I don't care."

"I think you do." Now she was starting to sound like Bailey and Jeannine.

"Thanks for your concern, Kelsey. But I'm fine. Everything is fine." I eyed her, and she gave me one nod, turning to leave the office.

An email from my head contractor was at the top of my inbox when I opened it, and I squinted, reading it three times to be sure I'd read it right. "Kelsey!" I screamed, and she ran back into the room.

"What?" She asked out of breath.

"This email says the project has been fully funded and paid up through the rest of the year." I pointed at the text from my contractor. "Did my father call?"

She shook her head. "Not once. He's out on the east coast I believe."

I searched the letter again for a source of where the income had come from but came up empty. "Could you find out who supplied these funds, please?" I pointed to the screen and stepped away from the computer.

I walked into the kitchen, reaching for my cell. My thumb hovered over my father's contact for a few minutes. Had he done this? Was this his way of trying to mend the burnt bridge between us? I hadn't spoken to him since I'd left the company and a rock lodged itself in my throat at the thought. I hit the button, and it only rang once before he answered.

"Paige? Are you all right?" He asked without saying hello.

"I'm fine, father. I called to see if you were responsible?"

"For what?"

"For paying off my contractors. For supplying funds for the rest of my project."

He sighed. "No, Paige. I had given that some thought, but I didn't want you to think I was attempting to takeover what you started. If you will allow me, I would love to discuss a way in which I can help. Perhaps even discuss you coming back—"

"I can't." I took a deep breath.

"Word is you haven't taken the position at Wilson and Rowe, yet."

"I'm taking some personal time to think."

"Good. That's good. You should." Silence took up the

other end of the line for so long I thought we'd gotten disconnected. "I am sorry, Paige. I've never regretted anything more."

Tears filled my eyes, and I cursed the hormones robbing my body of control. "That means a lot. Thank you, Father. I have to go."

"Can we have lunch when I get back in town?" He asked before I could hang up.

"Sure." I ended the call before I turned into a sobbing mess. I was still angry with him, but he was my father. I didn't want to hate him forever.

"Paige?" Kelsey popped into the kitchen, and I jolted against the counter at her presence.

"Yes?"

"I found out who supplied the funds."

I raised my eyebrows at her. "And?"

A smile played at the corner of her lips. "It was Rory."

My mouth dropped. *No way.* "You're sure?"

She nodded. "One hundred percent."

I stared at her without really seeing her. Funding my site was no small bill—it was in the millions. Sure, I knew Rory had more than that, but this? Why would he do this?

You know why.

That damned voice that was *so* Team Rory was back and whispering hope to my heart.

"Thank you, Kelsey," I finally muttered, glancing at the cell still in my hand.

Rory loved me. He actually loved me. And Jeannine had been right all along. About my need of the list, about my need of Rory, and about his need to force me away in some twisted sense of protecting me. That was the only explanation.

"If you'll excuse me," I said, pushing his number on my phone. "I've got to make a call."

She clapped her hands together before rushing off.

His number went straight to voicemail each time I tried to call. I glanced at the date and smacked my forehead. It was game four of the Stanley Cup Finals. The Sharks were at Ontario, which meant they were all the way in Ottawa, Canada.

I dialed another number. "Bailey!" I said once she answered. "What hotel are you, Gage and Rory staying at in Ottawa?"

"Four Seasons." She answered immediately. "Why?"

Giddiness bubbled up in my throat before being shot down. "Wait. Can I fly in the first trimester?"

"Yes. You totally can," she said, my expert mom of a friend. "But you have to take precautions. Drink tons of water, walk around the cabin as often as you can..."

"Okay," I said after she continued to quote statistics and risks. "Thank you!"

"Of course! Get here, girl!" She cheered as I hung up.

I rushed around the house, packing in a flurry of movements after I'd called to reserve the company plane. I was still a Turner after all.

An hour later I was on the tarmac, my hand protectively over my stomach as I awaited takeoff. Rory couldn't answer his phone right now. Fine. I'd come to him, but I was sure he'd known that. Hadn't I *always*?

———

After seven hours, we'd landed with just enough time for me to call a cab, make it to the rink, and pay a guard an insane amount of money to let me watch the last of the game. The Sharks won in a shutout and Rory was glorious to behold. He skated faster, hit harder than I'd ever seen him. He was on fire.

They were tied at two games each, which meant Game Five would be in Seattle. Home.

I couldn't wait another second before seeing him.

I pounded on the locker room door after they'd fled the ice. Screaming his name like a madwoman.

It only took a second for him to swing it open, rushing out of it without a shirt on and covered in fresh game sweat.

The breath caught in my throat as I locked eyes with his crystal blue gaze. I smiled at him, unable to speak, unable to move. His chest rose and fell rapidly as he took two agonizingly slow steps toward me before he sank to his knees. He timidly gripped my hips, and I sighed from his touch. Planting a kiss on my stomach, I gasped.

"You know?"

He stood up, towering over me as he cupped my cheek. "I know."

"And?" I asked, fear clogging my veins with ice.

"And I love you, Red." He pressed his slick forehead against mine. "I've never loved anyone else. And I'm sorry for—"

I cut him off with a kiss, unable to take a second longer where his lips weren't on mine. He gently lifted me to his level, stroking my mouth with his tongue like it was the last time he ever would. Pulling back, I gasped for the breath he stole from me, and he quickly set me down, his eyes darting over every inch of my body.

"Did I hurt you?" He touched my stomach, and I laughed.

"No. Rory, we're fine." I smiled.

He snapped his eyes up to me. "Are *we*?"

I bit my bottom lip, tears filling my eyes as I looked at the man of my dreams. I reached for his hand and squeezed it. "We are."

He sighed and kissed me quickly. "I should shower," he said but made no motion to leave.

"And get dressed," I teased, glancing down at his Bauer hockey pants.

"I don't want to leave you again." He pushed some hair away from my face.

"You won't." I shook my head. "I won't let you."

His lips crushed mine before he pulled back. "I love you."

"I love you," I said. "Now go. Shower. I'll meet you at the hotel."

He cocked an eyebrow at me. "You know where I'm staying?" he smirked. "You know, a woman once told me that stalking is only sexy in the movies."

I laughed, pressing up on my tiptoes to whisper in his ear. "Right. And lists are meant for groceries." I winked at him before turning on my heels and walking toward the exit.

EPILOGUE

RORY

THE CROWD ROARED as we left the ice, the spotlights spinning in a chaotic pattern, the music's beat pulsing with the blood in my veins. The pressure was on this season, and we'd just won our opening game. As defending Stanley Cup champions, we had everything to lose.

But I had everything to gain.

Like the eight-point-five million dollar a year contract I'd just signed this summer with the Sharks that guaranteed to keep me in Seattle for the next five years, and made me the ninth highest paid player in all of the NHL.

I sped through my locker room routine, while I joked with the guys and tormented the newest rookies, whose eyes were as big as saucers. No more goofing off, no more stalling before heading out to the bar. Game was over, and I had better things to do than hang around the locker room.

"Hey, you coming over this weekend?" Gage asked as I zipped up my bag.

"Barbecue at your place? We'll be there," I told him. Shit, we'd gone so damn domestic.

I exited the locker room and was immediately hounded

by press. I took two questions, both of which revolved around our newest rookie, Gentry, and how he was fitting into the house as our goaltender. A glimpse of red from over the reporter's shoulder was all I needed to wish them all a good night, and ditch the dog and pony show.

I pushed through the small crowd to see Paige leaned up against the wall, her hair piled on her head in some kind of knot, my jersey covering her gorgeous, swollen belly. Gone were the sexy pumps for the next—and last—couple months of her pregnancy, and in their place were adorable chucks that I tied every morning since she couldn't reach her toes.

"Good evening, my ladies," I said, kissing Paige's stomach, and receiving a kick for my effort from our little girl, whom we'd just decided to name Daphne.

"Hiya, stranger," Paige said with a smile.

I kissed her softly, cupping her face as I caressed her lips, gently tugging on the lower one. She whimpered slightly, arching up for a deeper kiss, and I briefly obliged. The press had long-since gotten over taking pictures of our PDA, and since I'd put a ring on her finger right after we'd won the Cup, we were old news to them.

That was me: Rory Jackson. Old, married, domestic, expectant father.

Never happier.

"You get everything done you wanted to at the office today?" I asked as I held her hand, leading her out to our car. She'd walked away from every job offer in order to run her own non-profit. Jackson Squared was her baby, now. We'd started it up with my signing bonus, funding not only the Seattle shelter but one in Oregon, too. Now Paige spent her days, and her energy doing what she loved—raising funds and making savvy decisions that made a difference in the lives of the homeless. I knew one day she'd want to return to corporate America, where she shone, but for now, she was happy and thriving while waiting for our daughter, for whom she'd already sworn off nannies.

"I looked at the plans for the new shelter in Portland, and the site for the prospective one in Sacramento. Ooh, and I took a phone call from Matt Donaldson, who wants to help out with sponsoring one in L.A." A devilish gleam crossed her green eyes as she leaned back against my very new, very safe, very family-friendly Range Rover. It matched the garage of our very big, very appropriate new home in Gage's neighborhood. Our kids would grow up together and have the kind of friendship and support I'd only ever dreamed of. "He told me that he couldn't wait to see me next month when he flew in and that the pictures he'd seen of me showed that pregnancy made me glow—"

I claimed her mouth, careful with our daughter between us as I pinned my wife to my car. I laced our fingers, holding her hands against the glass as I took her mouth the way I couldn't wait to take her body—with full, sweeping strokes of my tongue. Fuck, the woman drove me wild.

Months of anger management counseling had my temper firmly checked, but the jealousy always flared, and she knew it. She reveled in how much I loved her, worshipped her, and how much power it gave her over me. Since I maintained about ninety-five percent of the power in the bedroom—the way she liked it—I let her goad me whenever she wanted.

Hell, she could do whatever she wanted as long as she loved me.

"Tell Matt Donaldson that you're married and heavily pregnant with *my* child. And once you're healed, and strong, you'll be back under me, over me, bent over in front of me, so our daughter has a sibling. There won't be a day where I won't be inside you in some way or another, so you really have no time for Hollywood do-gooders. Besides, you're too busy doing good yourself."

Her smile lit the night as she brushed her lips against mine. "I kinda like it when you go all caveman."

"I'm well aware."

Her arms wrapped around my neck, her scent and feel already making me harder than the car she leaned against. "I did something else today," she said with a smirk.

"Oh? Do tell."

"Number seventeen?" she asked coyly, biting her lip.

"The swing?" my voice nearly broke on the last word, but I hung onto my manhood by a thread.

"Installed in our bedroom today."

"Holy. Shit." A swing. In our bedroom. No pressure on her belly, no worries that my weight would crush her...just pure, simple access to my wife, and the ability to make her scream.

"How about you take me home, Mr. Jackson?"

"Anything for you, Mrs. Jackson."

God, I loved this woman. Her mind, her heart, her soul. She'd be the mother to our daughter that I hadn't had. I'd be the father who would crush anyone who looked at my baby girl sideways. We'd be a family—and we'd have forever.

THE SEATTLE SHARKS HAVE BITE!

Sign up here for my newsletter for exclusive content and giveaways!

Follow me on Amazon here to stay up to date on all upcoming releases!

ABOUT THE AUTHOR

Samantha Whiskey is a wife, mom, lover of her dogs and romance novels. No stranger to hockey, hot alpha males, and a high dose of awkwardness, she tucks herself away to write books her PTA will never know about.

https://www.facebook.com/TheRealSamanthaWhiskey/

ACKNOWLEDGMENTS

Thank you to my incredible husband and my awesome kids without which I would live a super boring life!

Huge thanks must be paid to these amazing authors who have always offered epic advice and constant support! Not to mention creating insanely hot reads to pass the time with! Sosie Frost, Winter Renshaw, Gina L. Maxwell, and Heather Stone...there aren't enough words for how much I adore each and every one of you!